Because of You

by

GWENYTH CLARE LYNES

Grosvenor House
Publishing Limited

This book is published by
Grosvenor House Publishing Ltd
28-30 High Street, Guildford, Surrey, GU1 3EL.
www.grosvenorhousepublishing.co.uk

A CIP record for this book
is available from the British Library

ISBN 978-1-78148-742-6

The characters, events and places in this book, other than Lowestoft, Norwich and Edinburgh, are fictional and any resemblance to actual persons, events or places is purely coincidental.

Any mistakes are the author's entirely.

Dedication

For Trevor, Clarissa & Richard, Jon & Toni,
Andi & Bev

With Every Blessing

Gwenyth-Clare Lynes

GLOSSARY

Inspired by Newtown, mentioned in Gillingwater's Mediaeval History of East Anglia, Newton Westerby has been placed somewhere south of the Norfolk/Suffolk border. This fishing port has long disappeared so today only exists in the imagination of the author and reader. The local inhabitants, who are native born, speak with a Suffolk dialect. However, only the Cook family and some of the older residents, have been depicted as using such in the text.

Suffolk people have a tendency to use double negatives i.e. won't be no more.

Ow/ou pronounced ew i.e. snow – snew.
O/ow pronounced oo i.e. so – soo, go – goo.
Aloan – alone.
Bor – boy.
Dew – do.
Doan't – don't.
Fule/fewell – fool.
Funny – odd/strange.
Fust – first.
Git - get.
Hen't – haven't/have not; hasn't/has not.
Ole – old.
Putter – complain.
Mardle/mardling – to chat/chatting.

Rud - road
Rum ole do – strange happenings.
Squit – nonsense.
Stuff – things of an uncertain kind.
Taak – take.
Tew – to.
Thass – that's/that is.
Thowt – thought.
Ul – I'll/ I will.
Wholly – really.
Worsent – worse.
Yew – you.
Yewsel' – yourself.
Yow'n/yourn –your/yours.

Chapter One

Mick Kemp propped his left foot on the milk crate he had just placed on the floor at the foot of the stairs. He rubbed his back as he unbent then looked up and greeted his youngest daughter with a playful bow and a flourish as she made her descent from the flat above the Village Stores.

"Happy Christmas Eve, Em, oh most glorious early riser," he jested.

"Happy Christmas Eve, to you too, Dad," responded Emma cheerfully as she bounced down the stairs, her arms outstretched to hug her father as she reached the bottom step.

"Don't be such a tease," she whispered in his ear as she kissed his cheek affectionately.

"Me a tease?" Mick grinned in mock disbelief. "Why, I'm up at this hour every day of the year, slaving away while you catch up on your beauty sleep. It's you who's a tease making such an early appearance on Christmas Eve; your day off to boot!" He buoyantly returned her hug then bent to pick up the milk crate.

"It was you who wanted me up early, to help with the Christmas orders and receive last minute instructions, before you and Mum leave for Edinburgh."

"Is that so?" Mick raised his eyebrows, "An ideal opportunity for you to earn extra pocket money, more like." He chuckled as he straightened up.

Emma stood with her hands on her hips, head held high, and stamped her foot. Tossing her rich auburn hair across her shoulders, she scolded, "Dad! Stop messing about! You know I'm more than willing to help out in the shop over the Christmas hols so that you and Mum can have a well earned break."

"Sure, m'girl," Mick retorted jocularly.

"Well, I do know Drew and Morag are really excited that you're actually going to make it this year," she wagged a finger at him playfully. Although the Kemp's Dentist son and daughter in law had been married, and settled in Scotland, for more than three years, promised visits had never occurred for various reasons. Predominantly, pressure of work in the Village Stores and the supposed inconvenience to the village community, if they were to close for any length of time, were the reasons frequently cited.

"Right then, mustn't let them down, must we? You'd best go eat the breakfast Mum's cooked before you make a start on all those orders."

"Oh no, Dad, not at this hour," Emma struggled to keep the groan to herself, her stomach revolting at the very idea of cooked food so early in the morning.

"My dear girl, you'll need it to get through this day. Before long you'll be rushed off your feet, no time for a coffee break. Nicky will be in at 8 o'clock to start deliveries, and Rosalie soon after, so we need to move pretty sharpish."

Mick turned to carry on so didn't hear the muttered, "Don't call me, dear," an endearment Emma detested.

"By the way, this crate is the spare," he said quietly nodding towards the load in his hands.

Emma's eyebrows shot up quizzically.

"You still carry on the old tradition, then?"

"Of course, someone always runs out. So, put it outside the shop door Christmas morning with this note," Mick nodded towards the card balanced on top of the crate. "Folk will help themselves as they have need."

"You're so thoughtful and trusting, Dad," Emma hugged her father again, crate and all.

"That's what Christmas is all about, isn't it? Reflecting on the birth of the baby at Bethlehem and trusting Him as our Saviour."

"That's not what I meant and you know it. How do you know it won't get pinched or trashed by vandals?"

"It never has."

"There's always a first time," retorted Emma, flicking her auburn head to one side, "and why don't you charge?"

"It's Christmas," replied Mick simply.

"Peace and goodwill and all that, then?" quipped Emma darting out of the way so her father could take the crate through to the cold store.

Clutching her coat closely around her, Emma opened the back door of the Village Stores, sucked in a deep breath as she prepared to brave the elements and rapidly crossed the yard to her parent's bungalow. The kitchen lights blazoned a clear pathway through the dark, crisp morning for her to follow. Through the window Val could be seen putting finishing touches to a full English breakfast. Mick heard the morning greetings between mother and daughter. How he loved them both. Val, his wife for thirty-one years and, because of her brilliant organization and culinary skills, the practical half of their business partnership; Emma, his independent, youngest daughter, *no longer a stroppy teenager,* he mused, *but an engaging young woman of twenty-one.* Emma was working towards her teaching diploma having already gained her degree in the Arts. *She still holds strong opinions but is learning fast to be tolerant of other's points of view. Thankyou, Lord, for Your miracle of grace.* She'd also retained her sense of fun and over the years built up a good rapport with the customers, first as a Saturday girl and then during school and college holidays.

Mick stroked his chin thoughtfully. *Yes, Emma will keep the customers happy, but she won't stand any nonsense.* He had no qualms about that, and Alex, his eldest daughter, would keep the books straight with her accountant's expertise. With Rosalie Andaman's mature experience to keep an eye on things, (she had been his assistant for nearly seventeen years) Mick was certain the Post Office and General Stores would come to no harm whilst he and Val took a long overdue holiday.

Villagers said the shop was the centre of village life and for over a century it had been a meeting place for gossip and exchange of ideas. It was the hub of village affairs where people gathered when something happened like the floods, loss of a boat, sea rescue or a fire. What was it Lord Edmund said? "It's the pulse that creates vibrancy throughout the whole village. Moves people to action!" he once bellowed.

Others gravitated to the Village Stores when there was news to share, a wedding, a birth, a newcomer or even a death. The lonely wandered in more frequently than most, more for company than provisions, and Mick had long discovered that Rosalie, with infinite patience and wisdom handled their needs with such delicacy that he left her to it. He was amazed how many times those moments of kindness led to unplanned purchases.

For the young the Village Stores had become a central place to "hang out". It was near the bus stop so offered opportunity to purchase stop-gap snacks in place of missed breakfasts on the way to school or college in the mornings, and with a wooden bench outside on the neat paved area, a convenient place to gather in the evenings with friends, park bikes, initiate romances or kick around a football.

Some of the community used it as a convenience store when they ran out of necessities and didn't want a trip to a town supermarket, but the more discerning lingered at the delicatessen counter or the whole food section or drooled over the mouth-watering delicacies conjured up by Val and her team. It amused Mick that holidaymakers, staying in their seaside village, were both astonished, and relieved, to find such a well-stocked shop so far from what they considered civilization.

According to the Historian, Gillingwater, in the Middle Ages, Newtown had been a large thriving commercial fishing port on the East Anglian coast of England. However, the ravages of time and ocean had taken their toll and Newtown East-by-the-Sea now lay under the relentless waves some three miles out to sea. It was said, by some, that at certain times the submerged Church bell could be heard tolling. All that remains, today, is the western part of that settlement, Newtown West-by-the-Sea, colloquially known as Newton Westerby, reduced to a dwindling fishing village surrounded by the inland hamlets of Newton Common, Newton Lokesby, Marsh Newton and Newton Bridge all struggling to survive an economic climate bent on wiping out small enterprise in favour of out-of-town shopping complexes on industrial estates in the nearby town of Lowestoft and city of Norwich. But the county planners had reckoned without the indomitable spirit of the local residents. *Yes, we're fighters, in more ways than one,* Mick reflected.

He straightened up and made his way to join his womenfolk for breakfast. He and Val had worked hard to upgrade the Village Stores to bring it into the twenty-first century without losing the character of the building, with its sense of history and "olde world" appeal. He had kept the Victorian windows on the Post Office side of the building but replaced the shop ones with large, airy glass panels to let in light and give clear visibility to his eye catching window displays.

He had also retained most of the wooden panelling, keeping the dark oak in the Post Office, whilst that in the Stores was painted pristine white. He used one shelving unit and a barrow from an earlier era to display organic produce and Mick sentimentally kept Val's Grandfather's counter just inside the shop door. On this was now placed the computerised till and the card PIN machine. *What would Grandad think of these "new fangled contraptions", as he would call them?* thought Mick. Behind it was still the lovely old shelving, once home to rows and rows of fascinating sweet jars containing humbugs and aniseed balls, gob stoppers, pear drops and the like, but currently displaying locally produced preserves and chutneys in front of antiquated metal advertisement panels and the mirrors used long ago to keep an eye on customers.

The greater incidence of shoplifting now was causing considerable concern. A clip on the ear and a quiet word from the local Bobby was no longer considered politically correct so he and Val had given serious thought to installing CCTV inside and outside the premises, linking up with Billy Cooper, the butcher across the road, for improved security.

Mick quickened his step as he heard Val call. Life had certainly moved on apace since Val's great-great-grandmother had opened the original Village Stores in the late nineteenth century. Change was inevitable but hard work was still a vital ingredient if the shop were to remain a going concern. He would go and eat his breakfast quickly then get on with the Christmas hamper orders.

Sadly, the future of the Post Office was another matter and along with other out-of-town postmasters, he was battling against central bureaucracy, who were determined to close the doors of village Post Offices. The residents of the five Newton villages were up in arms about the proposed closure and whole heartedly supported Mick's campaign to remain open and provide the service they required, "How'd we git ower pensions?" was the general cry.

Just along the coast a battle of a totally different nature was being fought between the wintry elements and a sturdy, well-laden, longshore fishing boat. With Doug and Dave Ransome aboard, the "Sunburst" tossed passed the lighthouse, and sailed into the calmer waters of the channel leading to the inner harbour of Newton Westerby. It was a reluctant dawn, held in an icy grip, that greeted their early morning arrival and for once Dave was glad to leave the turbulent sea behind them. He was keen to land their catch as speedily as possible, clean up the boat and help his mother, Christina, with the stall and deliveries, thus allowing him time to concentrate on his own preparations for celebrating Christmas.

During this trip Dave's mind had been very much occupied with plans for later in the day involving the delightful young lady who had captured his heart and with whom he wanted to spend the rest of his life. He had prayed sincerely for guidance concerning the right choice of life partner and believed in his heart that this was the future the Lord had planned for them. He and Jansy Cooper were lifelong friends. She shared his Christian beliefs and aspirations and her bubbly personality perfectly complemented his more contemplatative nature. *What a joy to be together for always! I'm sure Jans will agree.*

Jansy's father, Doctor John Cooper, was the G.P. for Newton Westerby and the surrounding area. The forebears of Dave's parents, Doug and Christina, had been part of the fishing community for many generations so Dave and Jansy had grown up together in Newton Westerby, attended primary school in the village, then travelled by bus to the City High School. But, it was not until Jansy commenced her nursing training in Norwich, as Dave was completing his time at Lowestoft College, that they were separated. Despite their many other friends they really missed one another and realised their feelings went deeper than mere friendship. The separation was more difficult to cope with than either of them could have imagined. They had been friends for so long, sharing many of life's experiences together through their formative and teenage years; always there for one another, supportive and encouraging, part of the crowd yet linked by an unspoken and undemonstrative bond.

At one point they were unsure how to handle the unsettling nature of their growing attachment so, on a weekend when they were both at home, they arranged to see Rev Hugh Darnell, their local Vicar. Hugh, knowing the young couple from their attendance at Church and involvement with the Worship Group Team and Youth House Fellowship, willingly listened. Then, with insight and wisdom, advised a prayerful dependence on God, their heavenly Father, for guidance regarding their future.

"And for the present?" Jansy's twinkling blue eyes earnestly held Hugh's penetrating hazel ones.

Hugh smiled. Jansy felt he could see into her innermost being. That he knew her every thought.

"One thing I've learned through the years is that God makes His will clear but in His time so, for the present, I suggest you use the time you are apart to learn the skills of your chosen careers and fulfil their demands with whole hearted commitment," Hugh urged.

"But when will we know His will?" Jansy persisted.

"God's timing is always the right time, Jansy, and all I can tell you is that when that moment arrives you will know."

Jansy rolled her eyes and sighed.

Hugh sensing her impatience inclined his head and with a smile said, "He's never late, you know."

Dave picked up her hand interlocking his fingers gently with hers, "Dearest girl, we'll pray and listen. Whether together or apart we'll honour Him in all we say and do, won't we, Jans?"

Slowly she nodded her head in agreement.

"Do you remember the words from Philippians 4 vv 6 and 7? "Do not be anxious about anything, but in everything, by prayer and petition, with thanksgiving, present your requests to God. And the peace of God, which transcends all understanding, will guard your hearts and minds in Christ Jesus." It's a good passage to keep in mind," encouraged Hugh.

"Yes, I seem to remember someone at House Group suggesting that when we are prone to worry over something we should turn those worries into prayers and let God deal with them."

"That's wise advice for all sorts of situations."

"Even ours?"

"Yes, even yours," Hugh smiled again at them both and Dave recalled how the Vicar had placed a hand upon each of their shoulders, prayed for them and then looked directly at each of them. "For guidance for each day, as well as the future, read your Bibles, for instance Proverbs 3 v 6 says, "In all your ways acknowledge Him and He will direct your paths." Don't just take my word for it. Prove His Word for yourselves. I make no promises that it will be easy or smooth; just allow Him to show you the right path to take."

They followed Hugh's advice and those quiet words had proved invaluable and a solid foundation upon which their friendship had deepened into love. A positive approach to their situation allowed their relationship to grow and their brief, infrequent, times together were all the sweeter and afforded much joy and happiness. Both looked forward with anticipation to the occasions when off-duty, college lectures and spells at sea allowed them moments together. Each was deeply aware of the sanctity of marriage and neither wanted to compromise or precipitate that sacred relationship so they deliberately met in public places or spent time in company with family or close friends.

Tonight Dave was going to ask Jansy to be his wife.

As the boat neared the quay Dave was jolted out of his reverie.

"Dad," Dave called out, "take the wheel. I can't see Wills ashore so I'll take the rope and moor up as you come alongside."

Father and son had a good working partnership and soon executed this procedure. They unloaded the catch and carried it along the shoreline path that led to the fish stall where Doug's wife, Christina, was impatiently waiting to sort out the orders and freeze the remainder of the fish. Most had been gutted and filleted whilst still at sea and she worked swiftly to complete the task anxious to be done so she could give attention to other matters. Her husband and son worked companionably in the boat leaving it clean in readiness for the next trip out, which would not be until after the Christmas and New Year break. While Doug completed the paperwork Dave strode to the stall, a song in his heart and a spring in his step. He was elated. Not long now before Jansy finished her shift at the hospital and he would be meeting his dearest girl.

As he approached the fish stall his eye caught sight of movement behind the wooden hut. Dave called out and walked round the back to investigate but couldn't see anyone lurking there or find anything untoward.

"Uhmm! Must be mistaken," he muttered to himself as he retraced his steps and entered the shack.

"I'll finish off here, Mum, if you want to go and pick up the turkey from Billy's."

"Thanks, m'bor, I appreciate that. I've so much to do. Most of the orders have gone, only Mrs Jenner's and The Ship's delivery left. Strange she's not been in. She's normally the first."

"If she doesn't come in before I've finished I'll drop her order in to her on my way home."

"Right, m'bor. Just that last box to put in the freezer, then scrub down, disinfect and all's done."

As she left the fish stall Christina mentally went through her shopping list, as well as preparations she still had to carry out for the family's festive celebrations. She made her way quickly along the quay to Billy Cooper's, the butcher in the village opposite Kemp's Village Stores, eager to get out of the biting wind that was stinging her face and buffeting her body.

The turkey's ordered, along with some beef and ham; mustn't forget the chipolatas for Mark and little Rhoda. Her grandchildren, who were six and three years old respectively, were spending Christmas day with Nanna Christina and Grampa Doug accompanied by their parents, Rachel, the Ransomes's daughter and her husband Ben Durrant. Mark would never forgive his Nan if sausages, his staple diet of the moment, were not on the menu. Dave and Jansy were joining them for Christmas Day tea, planning to share Christmas lunch with Jansy's parents following the Christmas morning service.

How good it will be to have the family all together, Christina thought, *the men ashore, relaxed, time to enjoy the grandchildren. No need to man the fish stall for a few days,* Christina sighed. *Whoo! What a relief. Ice-cream and jelly, in place of Christmas pudding for Mark and Rhoda; pork pie, make sausage rolls, finish icing the cake, wrap a couple more presents. Oh, hoover the lounge, clean the bathroom.* Christina felt a moment of panic that she would never be ready in time. Her thoughts were so engrossed in her list, and the tasks ahead, she didn't see Bernice Durrant as they arrived at the Butcher's door the same instant.

"'Morning, Christina," Bernice called cheerfully, "All ready for Christmas?" Christina jumped.

"Oh, Mrs Durrant, I was miles away. I'm sorry I didn't see you. No, I'm not ready. Are you?" she asked defensively.

"Yes. Just picking up my order from Billy," responded Bernice quietly. "I've only got the petits fours to prepare for the carol singers this evening, and then everything is complete. How about you?"

Bernice, wife of Roy Durrant, Newton Westerby's builder and surveyor, was the most organized person Christina knew. How ashamed she made her feel of her own haphazard approach to housekeeping. Her shoulders drooped, and she shook her head, deeply conscious of her own inadequacies.

"Oh, I'm just rushing to pick up my orders, then I want to get home before Doug and Dave so I can finish jobs at the house," she replied breathlessly.

Bernice turned to face her and said gently, "My dear, don't rush about so. I'm sure if you take your time everything will eventually be accomplished to your satisfaction. Relax, enjoy the day."

Christina's hackles began to rise. *Silly ole woman! What does she know about it? No smelly fish clothes to sort out and wash. No freezing cold working environment to contend with; she has no need to go out to work; her wages are not dependent on the vagaries of sea and weather; her husband is in a secure job. More than enough money coming in, even daily help when she needs it! Doesn't suffer stress and anxiety over the safe return of her family; only one, perfect, hardworking son, still living at home in their spacious, purpose built, villa overlooking the Green.* The muddled thoughts tumbled angrily in Christina's mind.

"Oh, but I've still so much to do, the cloth to iron…" she blurted out brusquely but Bernice, seeing Christina's furrowed brow reached out and kindly touched her arm.

"Don't fret so. I'm sure you don't need me to remind you to approach each task one at a time, complete it, then move on to the next one."

"I suppose so," she muttered ungraciously.

Bernice continued in a softly, encouraging tone of voice, "Instead of worrying say a little prayer and before you know it, all will have gone smoothly and in no time at all, you'll be finished."

Christina pulled her arm away angrily and turned to go into the shop but Bernice leaned forward conspiratorially, "Mick's got some delightful paper cloths, saves on washing and ironing, with napkins to match."

Christina sighed. Gradually the gentle, soothing nature of the small rotund Bernice worked its charm on her. Bernice smiled at her.

"Christmas is about joy and happiness not worry and tension, isn't it? Take a deep breath. Now, on you go and take pleasure in it."

Christina shook her head disbelievingly, and then looked into Bernice's kindly face, tears in her eyes, and impulsively hugged her.

"Thanks, Mrs Durrant, for those words," she gulped, "you're right, I am hasty and disorganized but in these few minutes you've helped me get things in perspective."

"I'm so glad, my dear."

"Not half as glad as I am that we bumped into one another. Thanks."

Restored by Bernice's calming influence Christina collected her order from Billy, picked up the groceries from the Village Stores, including an attractive holly design table cloth, with matching napkins, completed her tasks at home in a more orderly and circumspect manner and looked forward to spending a happy day with her family. *All because of you, Bernice Durrant,* she thought *but I wish you wouldn't always throw religious squit into the mix.* Then blushed when she remembered how she had almost flounced off in a temper ignited by Bernice's benevolent manner. That was just her way, with everyone. Bernice was always kindly, gentle and gracious, but straight, yet, there was not an ounce of malice in her.

Back in the Butcher's, early morning conversation centred on the route the carol singers would be taking later that evening and the refreshments each household visited along the way were providing.

"Well, I know Penny's serving fruit 'n spice punch and mince pies after the candle-lit service," volunteered Trixie Cooper, sister in law to Billy, the butcher, who was brother to her Doctor husband "and I'll prepare hot soup and short ..."

"'Scuse me ladies," Billy butted in, what's your order number, Bernice?" Bernice held up her order ticket. "Number twenty-seven," yelled Billy.

Pauline Cooper came through from the cold refrigerator into the shop carrying a large carrier bag. "Here we are Bernice, turkey, sausage meat, pork pie, bacon, sausage and a beef joint," Pauline reeled off the contents.

"Oh, and half a dozen eggs, please, Pauline," said Bernice.

"I hope you cherish this wife of yours, Billy, she's a real gem," commented a customer waiting in the queue.

"A great asset," remarked someone else.

"Never gets an order wrong," observed another.

"Always right change," called out a voice from the back.

Billy came to stand behind Pauline, placed his hands affectionately upon her shoulders and beamed at his customers.

"Yes, an indispensable asset. I made a good choice, didn't I?" he turned and kissed his wife's cheek, amidst the laughter. "Now, now ladies," he clapped his hands together, "who's next?"

"Forty- two," someone called.

"How on earth are you going to carry all that, Bernice?" inquired Trixie.

"I've got my shopping trolley here. See, it all fits in quite nicely. Thankyou, Pauline." Bernice took the eggs and placed them on the top of her provisions. "I'm off to make petits fours for the carol singers. What are you doing, Pauline?"

"I've made sausage rolls," she replied as she reckoned up the additions in her head.

"How much?" asked Bernice opening up her purse.

Pauline handed over the amended bill, "Please pay Jacky at the till. She's helping out today as we're so busy."

"You won't forget something vegetarian for Stephen, Annette and Hilary," reminded Trixie.

"Not much chance to overlook their tastes with Hilary around," Pauline smiled ruefully. "I've baked vol-au-vents and she's promised to make a mushroom filling and finish them off for me this morning, if she remembers to get up. Teenagers!" Pauline rolled her eyes to the ceiling.

"Intriguing how those three are vegetarians yet eat different things, the girls quite happy with salads and veg based dishes, whereas Stephen likes his pasta and pizza meals and occasional Quorn or soya dishes," said Bernice.

"Mmm! I can cope with Stephen's fads", said Trixie, his Mum, loyally, "but I don't know how Rosalie copes with the twin's preferences. They are so unalike. Annette keeps strictly to a veggie regime but there's no way that Nicky will give up his roast beef and Yorkshire pud or the delicious steak and kidney pies Rosalie bakes."

"Yes. It all started when they were in year eight at school. We thought it was a phase they'd grow out of but these three have stuck to it and now it's a normal way of life. Ironic when you consider our line of business," said Pauline as she weighed some ham. They laughed in response.

"Number thirty-four," shouted Billy passing another turkey laden bag to Pauline.

"Must get on! Happy Christmas," she smiled at her friends. "I'm planning to go to the Christmas morning service but not the midnight one so I'll see you both there."

"'Bye Pauline, 'bye Billy. Happy Christmas."

Bernice and Trixie left the Butcher's, their Christmas wares safely placed in basket and trolley.

"Roy and I are going to the Christingle Service, this afternoon, Trixie. I know we're not children but Hugh always makes it such a meaningful service and we get great blessing from sharing in the simplicity of it. I'm also looking forward to the carol singers coming round. Isn't Adam a superb singer's leader? Inspiring as well as encouraging," said Bernice thoughtfully.

"Some would say fanatical," replied Trixie tongue in cheek.

"They're starting off at Adam and Laura's aren't they?" asked Bernice. Trixie's facetious remark was completely lost on her.

"Yes, I think Laura's preparing a few dishes of nibbles whilst they assemble and they're finishing up at our house, by which time, I anticipate they'll be frozen and need warming up; hence the soup."

A cold wind swirled around them curtailing their pleasantries. Bernice tucked her scarf in more snugly and crossed the road to the Village Stores. Trixie put up her collar, waved goodbye and, along with other early morning risers, went on her way to complete preparations for Christmas, as the rest of the village tentatively stirred from their cosy beds and braced themselves for the chilliness of the day.

CHAPTER TWO

Further along the lane, within the sound of waves pounding on the shoreline, lights were switched on in a flint cottage at the end of a stark row of terraced cottages that had braved the elements for more than a couple of centuries. Inside, Rosalie Andaman shivered, and pulled her dressing gown more closely around her, as she turned on the kettle.

"Brrr! It's bitterly cold this morning," She walked across the kitchen, "I hope Melvin remembered to turn on the boiler before leaving for the sorting office," she murmured to herself but she didn't need to look because as she moved towards it she heard the boiler flare up. "Oh good," she exclaimed, then turned, and grasped automatically for mugs, bowls and cereal packets and set the breakfast table. Quietly, she poured orange juice, mashed tea and put bread into the toaster. She reached out to open her Bible for her morning devotions then glanced at the clock as her fingers turned the pages. After some precious quiet moments she thought about the busy day ahead and how she would be rushed off her feet in the shop and was thankful that most of the preparations for the family's Christmas celebrations were complete.

Her son's involvement in the Village Stores' Christmas deliveries came to mind and caused her to think, *it's unusual that Nicky's not put in an appearance.* Rosalie stood and listened. *I can't even hear him moving about.* She walked to the foot of the stairs and called, "Nicky! Nicky!" but received no response. "Come on, my boy, this isn't the day to be messing about; too much to be done."

After waiting and listening for a few moments longer Rosalie trudged upstairs and tapped at her son's door. "It's a quarter to seven, Nicky." She put a hand on the knob and opened the bedroom door.

"Nicky, you're going to be late." His mother moved towards the bed.

"Nicky, its time you were up. You can't let Mick and Val down, especially today." Even in the gloomy light instinct told her the bed was empty. She swiftly turned and switched on the light. "Nicky?" As her eyes adjusted to the brightness she cast them quickly over the smooth counterpane then put her hands to her face and prayed. *Dear God, where is he? Please let him be safe.*

Like lightening Rosalie moved across the landing and opened her daughter's bedroom door.

"What's wrong, Mum?" Annette, bleary eyed, was sitting up in bed having woken when she heard her mother calling her twin brother's name.

"Nicky's not in his room, his bed's not been slept in. Do you know where he is?"

"No, Mum." Annette jumped out of bed, grabbed her spectacles, and ran into Nicky's room.

"Where on earth can he be?" asked Rosalie, a catch in her voice.

"I don't know, Mum," said Annette quietly. "I'll get my mobile and give him a call."

Rosalie slumped down on her son's bed, bowed her head in her hands. Thoughts tumbled around in her mind. What had happened to reliable Nicky? He always said what he was doing and where he was going. "A better timekeeper than a clock," Melv teased him. What had changed this?

"No reply," said Annette after some frantic moments on the phone. "I've tried Josh and Stephen and some of his other mates but no one's seen him since about quarter past nine last night when, with Josh and Ryan, Nathan and Rosie he left Doctor Cooper's, so, I've phoned Dad and he's on his way home. He'll get someone else to cover his round."

She put her arm around Rosalie's shoulders.

"Mum, let's pray for Nicky." With a twin's intuition she sensed that Nicky was in danger but Annette's faith was simple and uncomplicated and she believed that, wherever Nicky was, God would take care of him.

At the Village Stores, Mick and Emma Kemp methodically made up the Christmas Hamper orders without interruption, while Val served the early morning customers.

"Smoked salmon pate, trifle and blackcurrant and lemon preserve. There, that completes Lord Edmund's order," said Emma placing the last item into a space in the box before ticking it off the list.

"This one's ready, Dad," she called to Mick, "only Miss Pedwardine's requirements to attend to and then I've finished."

"Right, m'girl. I'll just lift this into the van ready for Nicky to deliver, and then I'll give you a hand. I don't expect Jenny Ped's order will take too long to pack."

"Dad!" exclaimed Emma in mock horror at Mick's use of the children's familiar nickname for the recently retired headmistress of Newton Westerby's Primary School.

"Oh, I think you'll find she'll be less stiff and starchy now she's relinquished her position of authority. Always had to be seen to uphold discipline but, I think in time, we'll see her drop that officious mantle and the real woman who is Jennifer Pedwardine will emerge."

"I don't think so, Dad. She is implacable," his eldest daughter, Alex Castleton said emphatically, striding into the packing room.

"Good morning, m'dear. I didn't see you come in. You're early. What makes you think Jenny Ped won't unbend?"

"'Morning Dad, Em. She was in the Post Office yesterday afternoon posting Christmas cards and was quite indignant when I pointed out that it was too late for them to be delivered before Christmas, accused me of being lackadaisical and the G.P.O. of dissipated standards. And, it is not early. It's twenty minutes to nine," she said pointing to her watch.

"Good gracious!" Mick exclaimed with a start. "Where's Nicky? It's not like him to be late. Alex, just pop through to the shop and ask Rosalie where he is before you open up the Post Office."

"Rosalie's not here, Dad. Mum's in the shop on her own. It's frightfully busy but Aunt Bernice seems to be organizing everyone in that gentle, persuasive way of hers."

"We've been so engrossed in getting the orders correct and complete, I hadn't noticed the passage of time, nor realised your Mum was dealing with the customers on her own," said Mick.

"You and Em finish the orders, I'll go and ring Rosalie," offered Alex.

Emma tore the list in half and handed a portion to Mick. "We'll get it done much quicker this way."

Alex slipped off her coat and put it, with her handbag, into the locker room provided by Mick for his staff. She made her way along the passage intending to walk through the shop to use the phone in the Post Office. As she wove her way through the line of chattering customers the door of the shop was thrust open and Melvin Andaman burst in almost knocking her over.

Alex grabbed his arm and purposefully steered him through the archway into the Post Office away from the eyes of the gawping shoppers. He was breathless and obviously very agitated.

"Melvin, what's wrong? Where's Rosalie and Nicky? Dad's getting worried. I was just going to phone. As you can see we're awfully busy. Last minute Christmas rush!" Alex spoke slowly and calmly to allow Melvin to catch his breath.

"Nicky's missing!" he spluttered out with difficulty, plainly distraught by the situation.

"Missing?"

"Yes!" he gulped, "bed not slept in. No one's seen him since last night. Annette has a premonition he's in danger. Sergeant Catchpole's arranging house-to-house enquiries. What are we going to do?" He brushed his hand through his hair and Alex saw the anguish in his eyes. She gently pushed him to sit in the chair, kept in the Post Office for emergency situations, usually elderly ladies feeling faint or dizzy. Melvin bent his head into his hands.

"Rosalie is beside herself with worry. It is so unlike Nicky. Sorry to let you down. Today of all days!"

"What a dreadful shock, Melvin," Alex gulped. "I'm so very sorry but don't worry about the shop, we'll sort something out. You get back to Rosalie and Annette. Give them our love and assure them of our prayers."

Melvin struggled to stand up, despair on his face. Alex took hold of his arm to steady him. "I'll unlock the Post Office door for you then you won't have to push your way through the inquisitive stares of folk in the shop."

"Thanks, Alex."

"I hope it won't be long before you have some good news about Nicky's whereabouts. If we can do anything to help, just give us a call."

Hands in his pockets, head down, shoulders drooped, Melvin made his way home. Alex had never seen such pain on anyone's face. Nicky was a much-loved son and brother, a likeable, popular teenager in the village, level headed and reliable. What a distressing mystery!

Alex thought of Bethany, her adorable eighteen-month-old toddler, at home with her husband, Graeme. How devastated they would feel if something untoward were to happen to her. Alex involuntarily shivered. It wasn't worth thinking about. *Oh Lord, I pray for Your care and protection of Nicky. Be with him and assure him of Your loving presence. May he be found soon, safe and well.*

Hammering on the Post Office door shattered her private moments. Alex looked up. Josh Cook's face was pressed against the glass peering at her. Behind him a queue was forming. "Just a moment," she mouthed and moved towards the shop thinking, *I must apprise Mum and Dad of the situation before I open up.*

Val was still very busy serving customers at the till so Alex continued through to the packing room and conveyed to Mick and Emma all she knew about Rosalie and Nicky's non-appearance at the Village Stores.

Business like as ever Mick took only a moment to formulate a change of plan for the morning's proceedings.

"You open up the Post Office as usual, Alex, but put up a notice to say "Closing at noon". Emma, take over from Mum and ask her to come through here so that I can explain what's happened. We'll delay our leaving time to 1 o'clock instead of 10 o'clock. At least our suitcases are packed. I'll take out the orders; there's twenty-one to deliver. If you could stay on till about 2 o'clock Alex, I'd be grateful. I think the rush will be over by then so close the shop at 3 o'clock, Em, OK? I expect Mum will want to call in to see Rosalie before we leave."

Wordlessly Alex and Emma nodded and went to fulfil his wishes.

Alex wrote the closing notice and unlocked the Post office door. Josh Cook was first inside.

"Doan't yew know it's freezing out there?" He made to push passed Alex but she forestalled him.

"Oh, Josh, would you be kind enough to fix this notice to the window while I serve Mr Baxter?"

"Sure, Mrs Castleton." He completed the task then fidgeted while waiting his turn in the queue.

"Thanks, Josh," Alex said as he approached the counter, "What can I do for you?"

"Jus' collectin' Mrs Jenner's pension for 'er. She's a bit dodd'ry this morning," he said by way of explanation, giving her his most disarming smile.

"Go'rer card 'ere," he fumbled in his pocket.

"Put it in the machine. Do you know the pin number?"

"Yeah, she give it me." He deftly pressed the buttons on the machine and watched Alex counting out the money.

"Three weeks, 'er said," he reminded Alex.

He pocketed the cash Alex handed to him and made to move away.

"Don't forget the card," she called. He took it and swaggered out.

As he reached the door, Alex looked up, caught a smirk on his face and experienced a dreadful sense of unease.

Josh, unperturbed by any misgivings Alex might have about his transactions in the Post Office, jauntily made his way around the corner to the entrance of the Stores. As he approached the shop door he saw the delivery van edging its way out of the drive between the back of the Stores and the Kemp's bungalow.

Change yow'n tactics, bor, he thought mimicking his father. So, twisting as though he had just left the shop, Josh quickened his steps away from the door and reached the van within the blink of an eye. He put his hand on the door handle. Not wishing to be confrontational Mick lowered the window.

"'Morning, Josh."

"Hi, Mr Kemp. Jus' 'eard Nicky's gone walkabout," he jerked his thumb back towards the Stores supposedly to indicate his source of information. "I'll give yew a 'and if yew like, it bein' Christmas."

Mick, surprised by this offer of help from such an unexpected quarter, allowed his judgement to be clouded by his keenness to get the job done and accepted Josh's gesture at face value hoping there wouldn't be any repercussions.

"Why, that's very decent of you, Josh. Hop in."

Josh scooted round to the passenger side and climbed in.

"Heard anything about Nicky?" Mick asked.

"Naah," grunted Josh totally unconcerned.

"Oh," said Mick, somewhat taken aback by Josh's off handed manner with regard to his friend's disappearance.

"This is the delivery list," said Mick, getting down to business, "tick off each one as we deliver. With the two of us working together we'll get finished in record time. We'll do the Close first. Name and address and what's owed are on the card at the top of each box."

Josh pulled his weight in more ways than one; humping the boxes of provisions from van to kitchen table in most instances; ticking off orders from the list and devising the quickest route around the villages.

Mostly, Mick dealt with the customers except where there were two or more in the same road. Many of the regulars enquired after Nicky, who normally delivered their weekly orders on a Saturday morning, and not wishing to alarm people needlessly, Mick brushed aside the questions as best he could promising to pass on the accumulating Christmas gifts to Nicky when he next saw him. All went well until the last two customers. Mick endured Miss Pedwardine's dissatisfaction that her order was incorrect, a complaint totally unfounded, as the items supposedly missing were ones he had placed in the box himself, and Josh reported back that Gordon Durrant refused to pay for the groceries. Mick raised his eyebrows.

"Quite stroppy 'e were," explained Josh. As Cynthia Durrant normally dealt with household affairs Mick decided to deal with the matter later rather than waste time arguing with his brother-in-law, Gordon. He really didn't want the day spoiling by Gordon's pugnacious attitude.

They returned to the Village Stores. Mick gratefully slipped Josh a £20 note for his unsolicited assistance. The young man grabbed it, fingered it caressingly along the edge whilst looking at it intently, and then folded it repeatedly before pushing it down into his pocket.

Mick parked the van.

"Coming in for coffee?"

"Naah! Fings to do," Josh replied as he thumped the roof of the van then stomped away, shoulders slouched and hands in pockets. *What a strange mixture that boy is*, thought Mick, *one minute cheerful and willing, the next moody and recalcitrant. Teenagers! I'll never understand them. I wonder if there's any news about Nicky,* Mick reflected as he made his way into the Stores.

Meanwhile, at another venue in the village Josh's family featured largely in someone else's thinking. At the vicarage Penny Darnell slipped on her warm anorak. She checked the food parcel she had just finished making up with Christmas goodies for the Cook family, then added a jar of hand cream and pretty headscarf, with Michelle Cook in mind, quite sure the hardworking woman would be given little thought or thanks from her family over the Christmas period.

Joe Cook was currently at home having recently been released from prison following time inside for aggravated burglary. Joe had become bitter against society, those with jobs and people he considers better off than himself, since being made redundant from the nuclear power station at Sizewell, further down the coast. He found it difficult to get another job but instead of accepting the offer to retrain had used his brain, certainly not his brawn, to organize crime; drank to deaden the memory of what once had been and blamed everyone but himself for his plight. Now, he was a bully, lazy, artful, attributing his criminal endeavours on all and sundry rather than accepting responsibility for his own actions.

Unfortunately, he was initiating Josh, his eldest son, as his partner in a life of crime, and many suspected young Bradley at eight was also becoming acquainted with the wiles of his father, learning to get through small window spaces, and pick up targeted items from homes, in a manner to avoid detection. The goods so collected were sold at the weekly Sunday car boot market held on Newton Common.

Michelle refused to help man the stall for Joe and the frequent bruises on her face were indicative of the treatment Joe meted out for her refusal. Maxine, at thirteen, had no such option and was ordered, along with Josh, to sell the ill-gotten gains from their father's exploits. The proceeds of which were spent nightly at the Ship Inn down by the harbour, with nothing going into the family budget, yet when he arrived home late at night, worse for drink, Joe demanded and expected a hot meal.

Michelle struggled to make ends meet and Joe's belligerence had reduced her to an anxious, thin, nervous, withdrawn waif of a woman at her wits end. Her once gentle, competent nature was completely changed. Their cottage was sparsely furnished but she worked hard to keep it scrubbed and polished. She had also done her best with the children, clothing and keeping them clean, feeding them nutritious meals on her limited income and teaching them manners and right from wrong but as they grew older Joe undermined and contradicted her all the while. Because of this the children were becoming out of hand, unruly, back chatting, and worst of all Josh was accepting his role of accomplice as the norm and enjoying it. So far Michelle had managed to shield five-year-old Thomas from Joe's influence. She maintained control of the child allowance and the wage she earned cleaning the school and Doctor's surgery, which enabled her to pay the family bills, but there was very little left over with which to buy extras to enable them to celebrate Christmas.

As she answered the knock on her front door, in her mind she was weighing up whether her resources would stretch to a chicken or if they would have to make do with sausage and mash on Christmas Day.

"Oh! Mrs Darnell," greeted Michelle with surprise, "come in."

"Hello, Michelle, I've come to wish you a Happy Christmas. I've brought a few things for the children which I hope you'll accept with my love."

Penny stepped inside with the parcels and noticed the chill of the house and the pinched, anxious look on Michelle's face.

"There's also some things of Ellie's that Maxine might like and one or two tops and trousers that Gareth has outgrown that might fit Bradley and Thomas."

Tears welled up in Michelle's eyes, unused to such unexpected kindness.

"Oh, Mrs Darnell," she whispered hoarsely, "thankyou."

Maxine beamed. She loved the trendy clothes Ellie wore. As soon as the boys saw the hamper they pounced on the chocolate selection boxes jutting out of the top.

"Cor, look Tom."

"Bradley," scolded Michelle, "put it back."

"But, Mum," he pleaded.

"Don't be too hard on them," said Penny quietly, "after all it is Christmas."

"No need for them to forget their manners," Michelle turned to the boys, "what dew yew say to the Vicar's wife?"

"Thankyew, Mrs Darnell," they chorused together sheepishly.

"You're very welcome. Enjoy your Christmas. You too, Michelle."

"Thanks," replied Michelle, "I am grateful for all this," her eyes glued to the unaccustomed abundance on her table.

"Is Josh alright?" asked Penny.

"Yeah, he's down the Stores helping out, so he says."

"I'm sure they'll appreciate that. They'll be busy today."

Penny moved to take her leave and at the door wished Michelle a happy and peaceful Christmas and invited her and the children to the Christingle Service later that afternoon.

"I'd like that. I will if I can get away," Michelle whispered, and then stumbled as Joe abruptly pushed her aside, having come into the house through the back door and seen the boxes on the table.

"What yew dewin' 'ere, Mrs High and Mighty? We doan't want no charity. Yew can taak yer cast offs back," he shouted as he threw the box of children's clothes at her.

"Dad," screamed Maxine, "doan't, I want them," and she scrambled to rescue the precious garments. He made to strike Maxine but Michelle rushed in front of her to protect her and took the force of his anger. He saw the bottle of cordial in the hamper, mistook it for wine not the hard stuff his body craved, so viciously smashed it against the corner of the table. The glass shattered and the liquid splattered on the wall, over a chair and the floor. Joe held the jagged portion menacingly in Penny's face.

"Posh, stuck up, la-di-dah missus, think yew can convert us tew yourn ways." He pushed her outside and slammed the door shouting, "Clear off, Mrs Dew-Gooder, and leave us aloan."

Trembling with fear and with a heavy heart Penny returned to her car feeling her visit may have caused more harm than good for Michelle and her children. She inserted her key but before she turned on the ignition she prayed, *Dear God of love and mercy I pray Your protection on Michelle and her children. May she know Your peace and love in her heart. Give her the courage to come to Church. I pray for her salvation. In the name of Jesus, Amen. How blessed I am to have a husband who loves our children, and me, and treats us with kindness and respect,* Penny reflected. *Father God, thankyou for Hugh.*

After sitting quietly for a few more moments she drove away to Main Street. *Must get on,* she thought, *I hope my visit to the Saunder's house will be less confrontational.*

CHAPTER THREE

Emma's stomach rumbled. It was almost lunchtime and the shop was enjoying a lull now that the brisk busyness of the early morning had subsided. She hoped to get a bite to eat but, she could see, and hear, two customers leaning over the desserts in the chill counter quibbling over the last trifle.

"Not much choice," mumbled one disparagingly.

"Thought they'd've 'ad more than this, it bein' Christmas," the other grumbled.

Then, they both reached out to pick up the trifle and clashed.

"Thass mine," Red coat grabbed.

"It's not, I saw it first," Purple coat shouted.

They each pulled at the container to gain possession, but in opposite directions. In the altercation the trifle landed upside down on the floor leaving splodges over the cabinet, their hands and coats en route.

"Now, look what yew've done," screeched Red coat, dabbing that garment with a grubby handkerchief.

"Doan't blame me. It's yourn fault for tugging so hard," retorted Purple coat.

Their voices reached a crescendo as Emma, who had viewed the entire episode from the counter by the door, approached them. She was seething.

"Now, now, ladies! Where's your Christmas spirit?" she spoke quietly through her teeth, fighting to keep her temper in check, and then pointed to a notice on the wall. "That has been on display since 1ˢᵗ November requesting customers to place an order if they require something particular for Christmas."

"Humph!" snorted Red coat.

Emma went on to suggest that, as they were both equally responsible for the spilled trifle, they pay half each.

Initially, Purple coat was speechless but Red coat caught her eye with a grimace and they united once again in their whingeing about the lack of choice in the Stores. But Emma remained firm and strode towards the till expecting them to comply.

Mick overheard the conversation as he took the route from the passage way, through the shop, towards the counter. He smiled to himself. *Well done, my girl. I wouldn't have had the nerve.* He was even more amazed at what he heard next and stopped in his tracks.

Emma said to the disgruntled customers, "As it's Christmas, to make up for your disappointment over the trifle, you may have either, the ice cream Christmas fruit dessert or the Madeira Christmas cake, for half price."

"Well! Thass very decent of yew. Doan't yew think so?" said Red coat, always one for a bargain.

"Uhmmph!" exploded Purple coat, her ample bosom rising quickly, and then settling slowly on her folded hands, as she declared in a determined tone. "Ul 'ave one of each!"

What cheek! thought Emma, but knowing it was Christmas Eve and any seasonal products left unsold would have to be put on sale at a reduced price after the Christmas holidays, or even thrown out, agreed. After all she wanted to keep their custom in the New Year and they were the sort of women who enjoyed a good gossip. Emma would rather they passed on good things about the Village Stores, better for customer relations.

The folk from Newton Common are a funny crowd, Mick thought, recognising the two scrapping customers as Dot Knights and Irma Morton, but the shop desperately needed their business, as well as that of the other Newton villages, to remain a viable retail outlet. However, he just hoped Val didn't hear that her delectable delicacies, which took so long to prepare, were being offered as a sop at half price to belligerent customers.

He and Val were ready to leave for their journey to the north and he'd come to say goodbye to Emma. Nevertheless, he waited till she had finished with the customers and they had left the shop with their bargains, before making an appearance.

"We're off, Em," he called out, not wishing to undermine her confidence by revealing that he had witnessed the whole episode.

"Ok, Dad," Emma replied. "Have a good journey and enjoy your stay with Drew and Morag. Give them my love and Christmas Greetings. Don't worry about the shop everything's under control and we shall manage." *At least, I hope so,* she thought with some misgiving as the enormity of the responsibility he was thrusting on her shoulders surfaced.

Mick put his hands on her shoulders and kissed her cheek. "I'm sure you will. I've every confidence in you. Because of your generous spirit Mum is going to have a complete break. God bless you, dear girl, and have a Happy Christmas."

"You, too, Dad," Emma smiled. *I just hope I don't let you down.*

"You'll be very much in my thoughts and prayers. Keep in touch about the Nicky situation," Mick requested, walking quickly towards the door.

"Yes, Dad," Emma replied sombrely," we'll keep praying for a positive outcome." For a few moments melancholy pervaded the air.

Then, Val bustled in and immediately her cheerful spirit lifted the atmosphere. She enveloped Emma affectionately. "Now, my girl, don't work too hard or stay up too late. Take time to enjoy this happy celebration with Alex, Graeme and Bethany, and the Doctor's family but remember to allocate sufficient time to complete your assignments for your course work. Don't forget to check fridge temps and sell by dates every day."

"Yes, Mum," Emma, agreed sheepishly, with a big grin on her face. "I'll do all you ask. Have a super time with my big brother. Happy Christmas." She reached up and kissed farewell to Val.

"Shop!" There was a shout and a rap on the counter.

"Just coming," Emma called. "Must go Mum. See you soon, 'bye."

Val turned to leave and then saw the mess on the floor. "Emma! What's this?" she demanded.

"Don't worry, Mum. I'll sort it. Off you go. Look there's Graeme with Bethany waiting to say goodbye to Gran and Gramps."

Having successfully distracted Val from the disaster area Emma left her mother to say her fond farewells to her eldest daughter and family, and went to deal with Mr Bracewell at the counter before cleaning up the trifle.

He paid for his purchases, then asked, "When yew openin' again?"

"Monday 10 o'clock till noon for essentials, then Tuesday and Wednesday 10 o'clock till three, look, it's all here," Emma handed him a leaflet from a pile on the counter. Other customers overheard their exchange and also clamoured forwards to take one. After perusing the notice for a brief moment one remarked, "You're not opening for very long, are you?"

"Well, it's an extended holiday this year with Christmas and New Year's Day falling on a Friday so Dad has done his utmost to cater for everyone. After years of experience he has a fair idea of the needs of the villagers."

"Yup, I s'pose so," was the reluctant reply.

"Well, if you think about it, school children and those on holiday from work won't be coming in early morning, will they?"

"Mmm, I s'pose not."

"And people with visitors or family arriving for tea prefer to shop, generally, late morning. Others, who've forgotten something or just fancy a change to Christmas fare, come in early afternoon."

"Yew be right! He wholly dew know us, to a T."

"Back to normal Monday 4th, then?"

"Yes, that's right."

"Happy Christmas."

"And to yew."

"See yew."

Alex had closed the Post Office at noon and completed the paperwork by the time Val and Mick were ready to leave at half past twelve. She stood with Graeme and a wriggling Bethany to wave them off till their car was out of sight. Then, Graeme kissed Alex affectionately before crossing the road to pick up the turkey from Billy Cooper's, after which he cheerfully sauntered home in time for Bethany's nap, wishing all he met a Happy Christmas.

Alex, meanwhile, returned to the Stores to assist Emma but no sooner had she entered through the door than Miss Pedwardine accosted her.

"Alex," her voiced boomed, "my order was short. Would you rectify it, please?"

Knowing how meticulous her Father and Emma were to detail Alex was sure this could not be so but she replied, "Yes, Miss Pedwardine."

Why does this woman intimidate me so and make me shake in my shoes as she did when I was at school? Alex thought.

"By the way," the retired headmistress continued, only slightly lowering her voice, "I think it would be more beneficial if you spent your time in the shop rather than outside it. You would then notice what was going on. I've seen a number of items going into someone's shopping bag and not the shop's wire basket." She looked pointedly to where Mrs Jenner was hovering by the shelves but directed her words straight at Alex, "What are you going to do about it?"

Alex thought quickly. "You may leave the matter with us and we will deal with it in the appropriate manner, Miss Pedwardine," she replied diplomatically. "Now, what did you say was missing from your order?"

A few moments later, Miss Pedwardine left the shop satisfied with the outcome, but Mrs Jenner was nowhere to be seen. Alex spoke quietly to Emma at the counter about Miss Pedwardine's suspicions that Mrs Jenner was shoplifting. The sisters agreed that it was a most unusual occurrence.

"I think we'll leave it for Dad to deal with when he gets home," suggested Emma.

"Yes, that's a good idea," replied Alex, "we don't really want an upset at Christmas." Yet, a thought niggled at the back of her mind that something had occurred earlier in the day that would shed light on the situation but try as she might she could not recall it.

As the news of Nicky's disappearance spread throughout the community, a steady stream of concerned visitors arrived on the Andaman's doorstep to offer support to the family and join in any search that might be planned. The phone rang incessantly and it was Annette who repeatedly answered the anxious enquiries concerning her brother as she remained far more composed than either of her parents.

Hugh Darnell, the vicar, was one of the first to visit and his prayerful compassion and care did much to alleviate Rosalie and Melvin's worries about the safety of their son.

"We may not know his whereabouts but our Heavenly Father is all seeing and all knowing. I believe He is aware of Nicky's situation. Let's trust Him to keep Nicky safe." As Hugh prayed, a calm peace came over Rosalie's heart and the tense anxiety which had held her in its grip since early morning seemed to fall away and she knew that all would be well, eventually. *Dear God, take care of my boy.*

Just as Hugh was leaving, Bernice Durrant and Sgt Tom Catchpole arrived at the gate together. Bernice was carrying a tray, full of food covered with a tea cloth, but the policeman was bearing a heavy heart because he was bereft of news following his house-to-house enquiries.

"Heard anything, Tom?" Bernice asked.

"No. Not a peep," replied Tom.

"How is it possible for an active, well known young man like Nicky to disappear without a trace?" Bernice looked up directly into Tom's face.

"Do you suspect foul play?" Bernice had the knack of saying what others were thinking but were too reticent to voice their thoughts, yet she always did it in the nicest possible way so never caused offence. The shadow of distress that crossed Tom's face gave Bernice her answer although he quietly replied, "I don't know what to think, Mrs Durrant, I really don't know. It be such a puzzle."

"Why, hello Tom, Bernice," greeted Hugh as they reached the front door, "I'm just leaving but I'm sure you'll be welcome inside if what you've got there tastes as delicious as it smells." He opened the door for Bernice to enter. As she passed him she whispered, "Just some soup and freshly baked bread." Hugh smiled. Were the occasion not fraught with such raw emotion he was sure the cameo of the tall lanky policeman by the side of the dumpy woman of goodwill would have been the source of much merriment. He turned to Tom and solemnly asked, "Any news?" Tom just shook his head.

Hugh reached out and placed his hand on Tom's shoulder, "I'm praying for you, Tom. May you get a lead, soon." Hugh's positive belief constantly uplifted his congregation and boosted their faith, too. Tom felt it at that moment, nodded, and silently blessed God for Hugh's encouragement.

Hugh prayerfully made his way back to the vicarage to make final preparations for the Christmas services and Tom thoughtfully followed Bernice into Rosalie and Melvin's kitchen.

Bernice swiftly had the family organized, seating them around the kitchen table to eat the delicious lunch she had so carefully prepared, before they realised what was happening. Just as quietly as she had entered their home with her kindness, so she left it, knowing that Tom Catchpole had some delicate issues to discuss with them.

Tom sensed a different kind of atmosphere in the Andaman home to the one that had prevailed in the early morning when he was first called. Then, there had been agitated bewilderment coupled with despair, now he felt, they viewed the situation with calm, renewed hope. Again, Tom thanked God for Hugh believing his godly influence had brought about the change. The facts remained the same. There was no new information, yet the knowledge of a caring community praying for the family, sustained them and enabled them to cope with the crisis in a more constructive manner. Tom gently went through his list of questions again, probing and sifting the information to see if there was anything he had missed or they had forgotten.

"According to Stephen Cooper, Nicky left their house, in company with Josh Cook, Ryan Saunders and Nathan and Rosie Jenner about 9.15pm. Did any of you see Nicky last evening after that time?" Tom looked earnestly at each face around the table.

"You mean when he came home?" Annette asked.

"Yes," agreed Tom.

"No," they all replied hesitantly.

Tom was perplexed. *Why didn't any of them see him? Why are they so hesitant about it? How can they be sure he came home?* Rosalie glanced at Tom and saw his puzzled frown and with feminine intuition suddenly realised they were not making themselves clear. So, in an attempt to rectify this she started to explain, "We all had an early start scheduled for Christmas Eve morning. Melv was on early shift at the P.O. sorting office, Nicky and I were due in early at the Village Stores and Annette was getting up early to do some chores for me at home, before going to Rachel Durrant's to have her hair done, so we all planned to go to bed early," she explained.

"Nicky didn't go to bed early?"

"We thought he had."

"Did you see him before you went to bed?"

"No."

"How do you know he came home?"

"We heard the front door."

"Did you speak with him?"

"Mum called out, "that you Nicky?"" volunteered Annette, as Rosalie suddenly seemed bereft of speech.

"Was there a reply?"

"Uhmm." Annette looked frantically at each of her parents. Reluctantly, Melvin responded, drawing his arm tightly around Rosalie's shoulders. "There was a muffled, audible sound that, at that time, we took to be a response from Nicky. We had no reason to suppose any different. We relaxed and soon fell asleep."

"What time was it?"

"I couldn't be specific but we started preparing for bed about a quarter to nine and we hadn't been in bed all that long when we heard the door. So if Nicky left Stephen and co. at quarter past nine I reckon it would be about half-past nine."

As Melvin finished Tom looked directly at him and the intensity of the moment was electric. In each mind lingered a nagging doubt. Melvin slowly lowered his shaking head in disbelief. During the course of Melvin's explanation there had been a rap at the back door and Christina Ransome, Rosalie's sister, along with Doug and Dave, walked into the kitchen.

Christina put her arms comfortingly around Rosalie's shoulders, "I'm so very sorry, Ros."

Doug shyly nodded at Melvin in his reserved way assenting to his wife's demonstrative display of family solidarity at this distressing time then leaned forward and spoke quietly in the Sergeant's ear, "Tom, can we have a word?"

The men withdrew and Dave acted as spokesman, "We've just heard Nicky's missing and come to offer our help. Would you like us to start dredging the harbour and scouring the beach? The Sunburst's all shipshape. It won't take us long to set sail and we can soon inform Titus Wills, the harbour master, of our intent. Your word, Tom, will add credence to our actions."

"Have you any reason to suppose we need to dredge the harbour, Dave?"

"No, not really, but I'll feel more use doing something."

"What do you mean, not really? We don't want to be engaged in something needlessly. Have you seen something?"

"No, not really," replied Dave tentatively.

"There, you've said it again," said Tom exasperated.

"C'mon bor explain yewsel'," encouraged Doug.

Cautiously, Dave explained the incident, or rather non-incident, of the early morning soon after they had landed when he went to relieve Christina from the fish stall.

"I saw movement out of the corner of my eye. I can't be more specific than that. When I went to investigate I couldn't see anyone moving or even anything suspicious and so I assumed I was mistaken."

"Now you're having second thoughts?" asked Tom.

"In view of Nicky going missing, yes, but as I explained I have nothing to base my hunch on."

Doug looked agitated; "But Dave, that's such a long time ago and the daylight will soon be fading."

"All the more reason to get started, Dad." Dave turned and raised his eyebrows questioningly at Tom. "Have the fishing sheds been searched?"

Tom nodded thoughtfully, "Go and prepare to commence operations, Dave. I'll phone and alert Wills, and then I'll arrange another check on the sheds."

"OK," responded Dave as he pushed open the door and briefly explained to the family, "Dad and I feel we want to be actively involved in looking for Nicky so we're off to help with the search."

"Dear God, whatever can we do," exclaimed Christina, as the men folk prepared to leave the house.

"We'll pray, Aunty Chris, we'll pray," affirmed Annette.

"Much good that will do," Christina muttered disbelievingly.

Pounding on the door announced the return of P.C. Prettyman. He had been to interview Ryan Saunders and Josh Cook with regard to the time, place and manner in which they and Nicky Andaman parted on the previous evening. The occupants of the room looked at him with anticipation anxious to learn any relevant information.

Before he could relate anything Sgt Catchpole's mobile rang. He answered it, and then stood up abruptly as he listened, moved towards the door and gestured to P.C. Prettyman to do the same.

"Right, Sir," Tom Catchpole nodded thoughtfully. The ticking of the kitchen clock pierced the silence.

"Yes, Sir. We're on our way."

He looked at the expectant faces. "No further news; another incident. We'll keep you informed and I'll be back."

The policemen made their exit. Outside, Tom imparted the news to P.C. Prettyman that there had been a break in at the Manor.

"Fill me in about Josh and Ryan on our way up there." As he drove Tom listened gravely to Dan Prettyman's report. "There does seem to be a discrepancy of about ten minutes." Suddenly he pulled up by the side of the road. "Is this the corner where Cook says they separated?"

"Yes, Sir."

"Let's check it out while there's still day light."

Treading carefully they noiselessly scrutinised the ground and examined the nearby garden walls.

"Sir, look," called Prettyman "there's a stain on this wall, and, uhmm, possibly drips on the ground."

"Blood?"

"Could be."

"Footprints here, and something," he paused, bent down and closely studied the ground, "a body, maybe, dragged across here."

"Tape the area off, Prettyman. I'll call the Inspector and request SOCO. We'll also need to see if the Jenner youngsters can corroborate the other's departure times."

After lunch Emma and Alex worked amiably together in the Stores. There were only one or two customers so Alex decided to cash up at half-past one and put the takings into the Post Office safe and carry forward any further receipts as petty cash to their next opening day. In between serving customers Emma checked the perishable goods. She was pleased to see there weren't many still in the chill counter. Their parents had planned meticulously and judged demand fairly accurately so that there would be very little waste. But then, they had years of experience.

"I've finished here," called Alex, as she locked up the Post Office and unless there's anything else you need me to do, I'll be on my way."

"No, everything's fine here. I appreciate all your help and glad you've stayed on. I'll wipe down the counters, sweep and mop the floor and lock up at 3 o'clock as Dad suggested. I'll also pop around to Rosalie's and see if there's any news about Nicky. I've one or two things to do up in the flat then I'll be round yours early this evening."

"We're looking forward to you staying with us over Christmas. Oh, by the way did Dad take Rosalie's Christmas order?"

"I don't think so," Emma slowly shook her head. "We didn't make one up for her this morning." She paused and thought for a moment.

"I seem to remember that in previous years, Dad usually gives her an empty box, asks her to fill it with all the things she would like, and then he takes it round to their house when he's finished for the day. I believe he adds a few extras and gives it to her as her Christmas gift."

"Yes, that sounds like the sort of thing Dad would do. Any ideas what she normally puts in it?" asked Alex.

"Not a clue, but I'll go get a box from the back-store now, fill it and deliver it after I lock up the shop," Emma called as she walked towards the storeroom.

Unless they hear soon about Nicky it's going to be a pretty bleak Christmas for them all, murmured Alex to herself when movement outside caught her eye. She looked up to see Josh

Cook and Billy Knights peering through the window. She shuddered and felt a sense of foreboding.

Emma returned with the box and they filled it with the most inviting Christmas goodies they had on the shelves but as Alex kept half an eye on the furtive actions of the two lads outside the shop she noticed the lights go out at the Butcher's across the road.

"I see Uncle Billy's closed."

"Yes, he normally finishes about half-past one on Christmas Eve, but then he's been open since about half-past five."

"Well, you've been up since then, too, so I think when I go you'd better close the shop, deliver Rosalie's hamper, then have a quiet couple of hours to yourself or you'll never last the night out, especially as you plan to go carolling and attend the late Christmas Eve service."

"Oh, Alex, don't be such a mother hen, I'll be fine," Emma chuckled.

Just as she placed the last item in the box the bell on the shop door jangled and Josh Cook sauntered in.

Emma looked up. "Hi, Josh."

Josh responded with a grunt, which she could only interpret as "Hi, Emma."

"Heard any news about Nicky?" she asked.

"Naah." He shrugged his shoulders nonchalantly.

"I thought you two were friends yet you don't seem very concerned."

He moved towards her menacingly.

"Yeah! Well, he'll be dead meat by now."

"Oh?" Emma said somewhat baffled by his words so she abruptly changed the subject. "You going carolling?"

"Might," he replied shuffling uneasily from foot to foot, then asked, "Yew busy?"

"No, it's quiet now so we're just getting ready to lock up."

"Took loads of cash?" He leaned across the counter, a leer on his face, sliding his hands together.

"Thousands!" Emma replied with a deadpan face. Alex, hidden by the display stand, gasped and sensed the situation could get nasty, so briskly moved to the counter by the till.

"Hello again, Josh," she said brightly. "All ready for Christmas?"

"'Lo, Mrs Castleton," Alex saw his shoulders slump as he dug his hands further into his anorak pockets. *Oh dear! He thought Em was alone and an easy target,* she mused.

"How can I help you?"

"Yow'n Mum and Dad got there yet?"

This was not the reply she expected so Alex laughed.

"Not yet Josh, they're driving not flying."

"Just thowt yew might 'ave 'eard by now. 'Bye."

In a flash he was gone and the door slammed.

Emma and Alex looked at each other and shook their heads.

"What was that all about?"

CHAPTER FOUR

Up the lane and across the Green, the Vicar, Hugh Darnell, sat at his desk in the vicarage. He looked out of the study window, but his eyes did not see Josh and Billy rushing by in the street, nor take in the ethereal beauty the crisp, frosty air was beginning to weave in the garden. In his mind's eye he could see the hills of Bethlehem where shepherds were absorbed in their daily occupation of looking after sheep, when their lives were changed by an unusual occurrence. An angel appeared in the night sky with a message concerning the birth of a special baby.

This Christmas happening was so familiar to many of today's Churchgoers, they were apt to be complacent about it, and never gave real thought to the meaning or wonder of the event. On the other hand, to others in society the incident was unknown so it never touched their lives. Both these factors troubled Hugh and from his heart he prayed that the Christmas message would be relevant to the people under his care in the villages this year.

Hugh had been incumbent at Newton Westerby for nearly three years. He had taken over from Richard Compton who, sadly, had been more interested in his own self-aggrandisement and social standing than the wellbeing of his parish, that most of the villagers were unaware they even had a Vicar. He made it clear his position at St. Andrews was of insufficient importance to warrant his full attention. His sights were set on attaining the higher things the diocese could offer. So, because of the lack of pastoral care, numbers in Church attendance went down and such wilful neglect of parishioners bred disinterest in the Church. Consequently, the arrival in the village of the Reverend Hugh Darnell, his wife Penny and their children Ellie and Gareth was welcomed with joy by the faithful, curiosity by a few and indifference by the majority.

However, in his first year Hugh faithfully visited every home in the five villages that comprised his parish, gave himself and his time to the people. Mere acquaintance was insufficient for his style of ministry, so he worked hard to get to know the villagers, their family relationships and idiosyncrasies and showed he genuinely cared for them and came to love them for Christ's sake. They in turn learned to love and respect him, and also took his pharmacist wife and the children to their hearts.

Stalwarts of the Church, Lord Edmund de Vessey, Val and Mick Kemp, Roy and Bernice Durrant, Titus Wills, John and Trixie Cooper amongst others, supported him, valued his listening ear and welcomed his forthright approach. An Alpha Course was started, invitations sent to everyone living in the Newton villages. A number accepted and through it many of his parishioners came to a new understanding of the Christian faith. Hugh's clear Bible teaching about its relevance to life today drew the attention of some people. The congregation grew but so did a desire to live the Christian life. It was not always easy and some struggled, but Hugh gently and compassionately encouraged them to care for one another in Christ's name.

On one occasion the Vicar suggested they pray about everything.

"What do you mean by everything?" they queried.

"Just talk to God about your daily lives as you talk to one another."

"You mean the ups and downs?"

Hugh nodded, "Anything that matters to you will be of concern to Him."

Some were sceptical; others declared it to be a "load of squit", but a number decided to "give it a go". The handful of committed faithful were encouraged in their own prayer life by the sincerity of the Vicar as well as altered attitudes observed in the lives of those who attempted to follow Hugh's advice.

He also commenced house groups to enable them to study the Bible, to increase their knowledge and understanding, and grow in the faith.

Thus, Christian activity was not solely restricted to the Church; there were vibrant pockets of prayer and worship, in homes throughout the villages, amongst all age groups. The pulsating heart of this community now stemmed from Hugh's study, his inner sanctuary, where he met daily with his Lord to recharge his batteries for each day's challenges, seek His will, prepare sermons, Bible studies and pray for the people entrusted to his care.

Quite a number of the villagers had enjoyed the balm of this special place when they'd sought a listening ear and were recipients of the wisdom and compassion from this man who walked so closely with his Living Lord. He made all callers feel they and their circumstances mattered to him.

"He hen't got his 'ead in the clouds, 'is feet be firm on the ground," remarked Peek, the verger, quite frequently.

"Yup, 'e not be full o' frothy ole squit," agreed Mrs Jenner.

Ben Durrant was heard to say, "Through the Village Stores Mick and Val Kemp supply sufficient to satisfy the physical appetite of anyone who cares to buy but through his explanation of the Bible, Hugh presents Jesus as the Bread of Life who satisfies, forever, the spiritual hunger of every person who, in faith, accepts Him."

Ordinary men working at an ordinary job, Hugh's thinking was still engaged on the occupation and demeanour of the shepherds, to whom the angel had spoken of the birth of God's

Son. *The shepherds responded positively to the news of His coming.*

In ordinary places Jesus still comes into the lives of ordinary people in ordinary jobs who respond to His coming in a positive way.

Hugh opened his Bible to John 10 v 10 and thoughtfully read aloud, *"I have come that they may have life, and have it to the full." That was His message to His disciples. That was the reason for His coming to earth.*

The phone rang. Hugh's train of thought was abruptly interrupted as he answered it.

"Hugh, Billy Cooper here. I've a spare turkey. Do you know a family in the parish who could make good use of it?"

"Why, Billy, that's very generous of you. Penny's out delivering the last of the food hampers to the neediest of the parish at the moment but I'm sure she will know of someone who would really appreciate such a gift."

"I'll bring it in when I drop off Jacqueline for the Christingle service. Will that be soon enough, Hugh?" asked Billy.

"Yes, that will be fine, Billy, thankyou. God Bless you and a Happy Christmas."

Having completed the tasks in the storeroom, Emma loaded Rosalie's hamper into the van, locked up the Village Stores and made her way to the Andaman's home. She drove carefully down Main Street mindful of the icy conditions. Dad would not be pleased if she damaged the van.

It was unusually quiet; few people seemed to be about. The descending gloom of a December afternoon coupled with the settling frost on the bare branches of trees and hedgerows made for an eerie appearance enough to send all but the hardiest of individuals back into the warmth of their homes.

Emma turned up the van heater and was relieved when, within a short time, she was able to pull into the pebbled driveway by the side of Rosalie's end-terrace cottage. She walked quickly with her heavy load to the back door, which was the nearest, knocked with her foot, manoeuvred the handle with her elbow, prepared to push the door open and call out "It's only me Rosalie," when the door was pulled open sharply and she stumbled into the arms of Melvin Andaman as he was about to step outside the house for a breath of fresh air.

"Ooops," Emma gulped, trying to regain her balance.

"Sorry, Emma, you alright?" asked Melvin concerned, relieving her of her load.

"Yes, thanks Melvin. I've just brought Rosalie's Christmas hamper. Any news about Nicky?"

"Not yet."

"I'm so very sorry."

Emma only stayed a short while before driving home satisfied there was nothing else she could do for her friends but pray. She was glad when she reached the door of her flat above the Village Stores. She had planned to do so much but once inside she kicked off her shoes, flopped down on the sofa and in a short space of time was fast asleep.

Meanwhile, Alex, too, had arrived home weary from the Post Office and Stores. Graeme greeted her warmly but sensing her tiredness sat her down and made her a cup of tea.

"Bless you, sweetheart, I needed that."

Together, they discussed the events of the day, while Bethany played happily on the playmat with some toys. Alex shared her misgivings about her dealings with Josh Cook and mentioned the episode with Miss Pedwardine concerning Mrs Jenner.

"I think you've made the right decision to leave it till after Christmas or let your Dad sort it out when he returns home."

"Maybe, although I think Em could have dealt with it. She is so straight and level headed these days, but to be honest we were both tired and felt it was best to deal with the matter later. Mrs Jenner's behaviour is so out of the ordinary. In fact there seems to have been a string of unusual incidents all day. The Nicky situation is the worst. Again, it's so out of character.

Melvin's despair was awful. It was such a shock, I didn't know what to say," Alex sobbed and tears coursed down her cheeks.

Graeme drew her gently into his arms and she rested her head upon his shoulder. His hand soothed her brow. "I'm sure you handled it calmly and sensitively, saying just what was needed, in the caring way that only you can."

"Mmm," she softly sighed and gradually her eyes began to get heavy. Graeme felt her body sag against him and soon she was fast asleep and he reached out to rescue the teacup before it fell from her relaxed hand.

While Bethany played, and Alex slept, Graeme sat contentedly in the presence of the two women in his life. His heart surged with love for them both. *O Lord, how I value every moment spent with these my loved ones.* With a father's pride he delighted in his little daughter with her dark brown eyes, chubby cheeks and fair hair, faintly tinged ginger. She brought him her favourite, squashy, squeaky doll and chatted away to him in her unintelligible gibberish. She knew what she meant even if he didn't. In recent weeks words such as Dadda and No were becoming recognisable. How his heart had soared when she first said "Dadda" to him. It rapidly plummeted when he saw her put up her arms to Mick, his father-in-law, and say the same.

Alex, his beloved Alex, had infinite patience with this precious gift who was theirs. What joy she had brought to them. He couldn't believe the love he and Alex shared could be improved upon and yet it seemed to get better and more deeply enriched as each day passed. He kissed the top of her sleeping head. Gentle, sensitive Alex, whose unswerving faith had influenced the direction of his life beyond all recognition. She was so beautiful. Her quiet spirit radiated the presence of God in her life and gave evidence of the beauty within her. When they first met it had fascinated him. He couldn't ignore it try as he might.

Alex explained simply how she had accepted Jesus Christ as her Saviour and pointed out to him his need to acknowledge his sins before God. If he didn't want to go to hell he needed to accept God's forgiveness and look forward to spending eternity in His presence. When he had attempted to argue with her she quietly opened her Bible and directed his attention to verses that challenged his heart, for instance, "All have sinned and fall short of the glory of God..." recorded in Romans 3 v 23 and "No one can see the kingdom of God unless he is born again," found in John 3 v 3.

"There is a couplet written in my autograph book many years ago by a godly man in our Church which I have never forgotten. It's based on John 3 v 16, "God loved and gave, we believe and live." Simple but true."

How Graeme blessed the day when they had quite literally bumped into one another, he drenching Alex with hot coffee as he turned too quickly from the canteen counter to take a seat at one of the tables, during a coffee break. They were both attending an advanced accountant's course at the University. Her startling blue eyes and vivid auburn hair caught not only his eyes but also his heart. Her gracious smile, and the pleasant way she dismissed the incident, drew from him a desire to know her more. With red hair like that he'd expected sparks to fly. *Seven years ago now, and next April we celebrate our fifth wedding anniversary,* he thought.

His eye caught sight of the clock.

"Well, little lady," he exclaimed to Bethany who was beginning to get fidgety, "I think it's time to get some tea ready. We'll leave Mummy to sleep." Graeme eased himself up from the sofa and gently placed Alex's head on a cushion.

He playfully scooped up Bethany and took her through to the kitchen and fastened her into the high chair. Whilst his hands were engaged in preparing and supervising his daughter's tea his methodical mind was cataloguing and rearranging the subject matter of Alex's day, particularly the Mrs Jenner scenario. *If she was too ill to collect her pension at nine o'clock why was she in the Stores at half-past twelve shoplifting? Also, why did she ask Josh Cook to collect her pension and not one of her neighbours? Or did she?* He would have been most surprised to learn Mrs Jenner was, at that very moment, huddled by a radiator in the Church, cold hungry and very distraught.

Down at the quayside there was a hive of activity. In record time Doug and Dave Ransome had gathered together additional equipment they might need to carry out their distressing task. Willing hands, eager to offer support or help in any way they could, assisted in hauling it aboard, rigging up a searchlight to give better visibility when darkness fell, and prepared to cast off.

Dave, who had donned his wet suit, "just in case," he explained, went to check the dinghy, its launching arm, the lines and the life belts. He lifted the tarpaulin from the dinghy, and then froze in horror, the blood draining from his face.

At a quarter to five Rev Hugh concluded the Christingle Service then stood in the porch of the Church to wish God's blessing and a Happy Christmas to the excited groups of children and their families, as well as some senior citizens, as they departed for home.

"Lovely service, Vicar," Laura Catton expressed thanks and good wishes for Christmas, whilst her children danced in lively anticipation around her.

"Look, Vicar, I've already eaten the sweets," said Daniel, skipping and wafting his Christingle in front of Hugh.

"I hope you enjoyed them."

"I'm not going to eat mine," Kirsten told him solemnly.

Hugh bent down to talk to her. "What will you do with it?"

"I'm going to put it on the table and ask Mummy to light the candle. Then, I shall look at it as I eat my tea, and see how pretty it is."

"As you enjoy your tea, and your Christingle, perhaps you could think of another little girl who is five, like you." Hugh reached into his inner pocket and pulled out a small photograph. "Look, this is Anekwe. She lives in a small village in Zimbabwe. Today, tomorrow and every other day, she will have one bowl of rice to eat."

Kirsten remained silent. She just stared at the photo. Daniel, who had heard the Vicar's last few words, stood still.

"Not even Christmas Dinner?" he asked in disbelief.

"Not even Christmas Dinner," Hugh confirmed.

"But, you said the orange is like the world. You said God gives food for the world that's why the Christingle has fruit and sweets and these funny black smelly things, to remind us, so, why isn't she getting Christmas Dinner?" The seven year old challenged Hugh and looked directly at him.

Kirsten looked intently at her Christingle, then back at the photo.

Hugh thought carefully before replying. "Food is not so readily available in some parts of the world and Anekwe lives in a very poor village where the harvest has failed because the weather has not been good for the food crops. They depend on other people from wealthier places to help them out."

"Then I'll save them some of my Christmas Dinner," Daniel declared.

"Oh, Daniel, what a generous thought," Hugh said as he ruffled the boy's hair then quietly added, "If only that were possible."

A group of people, waiting to shake hands with Hugh and exchange Christmas Greetings with his family, had stopped to listen to the unfolding conversation with the Catton children, smiled at the spontaneity of Daniel's response.

"Come along children, tea-time, the Vicar needs to speak to all these people," said Laura, holding on to a now wriggling Poppy.

Kirsten still clutched the photo. She looked up at Hugh. "I'll put this on the Christmas tree and say my prayers for her."

"Bless you, Kirsten," said Hugh, a lump rising in his throat at her childish simplicity, and he placed a hand gently on her head in blessing. "A Happy Christmas to you all," his broad smile encompassed each one, as they went reluctantly with Laura down the churchyard path, through the lytch gate and along the lane home.

A hand clasped his arm.

"A delightful service, Hugh, so full of blessing, thank you."

He turned and saw Bernice and Roy Durrant leaving the Church.

Roy dropped a hand on his shoulder, "That little incident was the icing on the cake."

"Goodbye, Vicar."

"Happy Christmas."

"See you later."

"A good afternoon, very meaningful."

The air rippled with goodwill. Soon the porch cleared of well-wishers allowing Hugh and Penny, with Ellie and Gareth, to stroll across to the vicarage to make last minute preparations for the Christmas Eve and Christmas morning services. Hugh engaged in precious moments of prayer in his study while Penny made fruit punch and set out mince pies, in the kitchen, for the carol singers and worshippers who would attend the late night candle-lit service.

Ellie and Gareth went to the sitting room to put finishing touches to the Christmas tree adding their own gifts to those already encircling the tree. Ellie was rather vexed because she wasn't allowed to go out with the carol singers. "It's really not fair. I'd much rather go carolling than attend the stupid, babyish Christingle service. Oh, Mum, please let me go," she pleaded.

"Ellie, we've been through all this before and you know the reasons for you not going carolling this year but I'm quite shocked at your attitude to the Christingle Service," replied Penny patiently, then quietly pointed out that the Christian message contained in the simple symbolism of the Christingle was for all people, young and old.

"Wasn't there a mix of people in the Church this afternoon?"

Ellie, with her head hung low, ungraciously agreed but determined to make her point added "that complaining Mrs Jenner was there and…"

"But she didn't talk to us at all today," butted in Gareth.

"…scruffy, smelly Mr Baxter in his dirty coat and holey socks pushed passed us on his way out, and those dreadful boys from the Marsh gobbled the sweets and even ate the oranges, before Dad had finished the service."

"Oh, Ellie, don't be so unkind. You disappoint me. They were probably hungry." Picturing the home she had called at earlier in the day and the slovenly approach to the children's needs Penny thought that was more than likely. She stilled her hands and gazed at her daughter who was struggling to look her mother in the eye.

"Mrs Jenner lives alone and is probably so lonely and appears to always be complaining to everyone she meets because she has no one at home to talk to or share her feelings and opinions with. Mr Baxter, as you know, lives on his own and has no one to wash and iron for him or remind him when to take his coat to the cleaners or comb his hair before he goes out. You and Gareth are fortunate that you have Dad and me to help you with those things." Penny paused for a moment to let her words sink in then asked, "Who washes your clothes, Ellie?"

Frowning she lifted her eyes, "You do."

"Who prepares your meals?"

"You do." She shrugged her shoulders. "OK, I get the picture. I'm sorry Mum," Elle mumbled.

"We do have each other don't we," said Gareth eager to add his pennyworth to the exchange, "and you always tell me when to comb my hair and brush my teeth and wash my hands and all the other things."

"We don't have chance to forget, "Ellie muttered.

"Oh, Ellie, my dear girl," Penny reached out and put her arms around Ellie's shoulders, drew her close and gave her a hug. "We help each other because we love one another. We are so blessed." She rested her chin on the top of her daughter's head for a loving moment then gently turned her round to face her. "I have to pop out for a few minutes but when I get back we'll continue our chat. Gareth, will you knock on the study door and tell Dad I'm just off to deliver the turkey to the Cook's house, thankyou. There's a Shepherd's pie in the oven, please keep an eye on it, Ellie. We'll eat as soon as I get home. I won't be long."

On her way Penny passed a police car going in the opposite direction. Unbeknown to her it was en route to the Manor.

As the police car pulled up outside the Manor House Tom Catchpole received a further call on his mobile phone. The stern grimace on his face indicated to P.C. Prettyman the seriousness of the call. After a few intense moments listening to the caller Tom looked up and mouthed "Dave Ransome."

"Mmm... Right, Dave, tell no one. I repeat say nothing of this to anyone. Stay there. I'll send P.C. Prettyman straightaway, get back up and an ambulance."

He turned to Prettyman. "Right, lad, off you go to the Quay. Dave's boat; He's found something. Keep everyone else away. I'll ask for silence from the ambulance crew so watch out for them, and direct them. I'll see to preliminaries here," he indicated the Manor House, "and join you ASAP. You take the car, I'll cadge a lift. No sirens. If SOCO are on site at Sparham's Corner take one of them with you and send someone up here. I know it's Christmas Eve but the sooner we sort all this out the sooner we'll all be home."

Tom got out of the car, made his phone calls, and then strode purposefully to the front door of the Manor as the young constable drove quickly down to the quayside.

Across the other side of the village Penny Darnell delivered Billy Cooper's spare turkey to the Cook's house. Michelle could hardly contain her surprise or delight at so generous a gift. It would enable her family to enjoy a sumptuous Christmas feast such as they'd not had for many years.

As she departed from the house Penny unwittingly caught snatches of conversation coming through the open kitchen door. She recognised the voices as those of Joe and Josh but couldn't make sense of what they were saying.

"Up his nibs, bottom kitchen all ok?"

"Yeah. All clear till later."

"'ow baht bonce bor?"

"Dead meat."

"Yew mean nuffin'?"

"Yeah, absolutely nil."

"Amazin'!"

Penny was concentrating so intently on the incomprehensible dialogue she didn't realise she had paused in full view of the chatting men. Josh saw her and nodded at Joe, who, believing she had overheard their chat was up like a shot. He raised his fist and hit her with such force that she crumpled in a heap on the ground. Her head struck the corner of the house wall and she fell awkwardly on her left arm. Joe bent over her and saw she was unconscious.

He signalled Josh to grab her under the arms and assist him to drag her to the car. Together they bundled her in and Joe drove to Doctor Cooper's. Silently they dumped her body in the porch way of his house. They sped off, the wheels spinning on the icy surface as Joe put his foot down, anxious to put distance between themselves and Mrs Darnell. However, the wound in Penny's head was bleeding profusely and one of her assailants had inadvertently acquired blood on his trainer and left an indelible mark on the step at the Doctor's, as well as, a tell-tale footprint and trail of blood outside their own back door.

Meanwhile, at the Manor the lanky legs of Tom Catchpole were striding out behind the upright figure of Lord Edmund de Vessey as they examined each room for signs of intrusion. Lord Edmund stopped abruptly as they approached the beautiful balustrade staircase, which rose gracefully from the spacious hall. He brushed a hand reflectively through his thick but greying hair.

"Tom, I'm puzzled. I can see nothing to corroborate trespass in any of the downstairs rooms other than the kitchen and the small sitting room."

"I agree, Sir. There's definite evidence that someone has climbed through the lower casement of the kitchen window. There be a distinct footprint on the window sill, and another be on the parquet flooring leading to the sitting room."

Lord Edmund distractedly shook his head in disbelief. "If only Lettie were here. She would know immediately if anything were moved or misplaced. But with Nicholas missing it would have been churlish of me to refuse her request to go and see her family. In fact, Sergeant, alongside that issue my troubles are trivial."

"What time do you expect Mrs Milner home, Sir?" Tom asked, thinking that Lord Edmund might be an astute businessman but he seemed less than observant about the home. *I guess that was the late Lady de Vessey's domain and he now leaves it to his housekeeper.*

"About five o'clock I would think. She likes to serve the evening meal at six thirty to oblige me. She is very conscientious so she won't be late."

"Right, Sir. I think I'll...." His mobile rang. "Excuse me, Sir."

"Oh, no!" an involuntary exclamation fell from Tom's lips as he listened to the caller.

"Right, Doc."

"Good! I have a SOCO team already working in the village. I'll send them along as soon as they are available. Doctor, this be a delicate matter but I know I can trust your integrity. Four incidents have now occurred. I believe they are linked. My boss be on his way, but till he arrives, I ask you to keep schtum."

"No, I'll see the Vicar."

Lord Edmund unavoidably listened to the one sided conversation and realised the import of the information Sgt Catchpole was receiving.

"Tom, you've obviously got a lot of calls to make, come and sit in the study and make them from there." As he led Tom through to the study they heard the back door open. "You go on in, that will be Lettie. I'll explain everything and get her to look closely in the kitchen and sitting room for anything amiss. If there's anything else I can help with...?" The question hung in the air.

While Tom made his calls, Lettie Milner, housekeeper to Lord Edmund, thoroughly checked the house and quickly noted that a number of small electrical appliances were missing from the kitchen, and cut crystal vases, bowls and ornaments as well as two inlaid mother of pearl photograph frames were absent from the sitting room. She was methodically writing a list when Tom came through after completing his calls.

"Mrs Milner, may I take your statement later and can I request that you don't touch the kitchen window or clean up the marks on the sill or the floor. One of the SOCO team will be here shortly to take photos and check all prints for evidence. Above all, please, for the time being do not discuss this with anyone."

The Sergeant turned to Lord Edmund, "Sir, my constable had to attend another incident so I don't have a vehicle. As time is of the essence could I ask you to drive me to Doctor Cooper's, the vicarage and then on to the quay?"

"Certainly, my man," and made ready to be off.

CHAPTER FIVE

❖

Back at the flat above the Stores Emma slept peacefully totally unaware of the disturbing events that were unravelling in the village around her. When she eventually awoke dusk had fallen. Darkness seemed to envelope her and for some moments she felt disorientated. She switched on the light and gradually accustomed her eyes to the brightness, remembered the day, and gathered herself together. She showered to freshen herself after the busyness of the day and made preparations for the time she was going to spend with family and friends over the Christmas holiday. Carefully she wrapped presents for the Doctor's family whom she was visiting on Boxing Day.

It will be good to see Jansy again, Emma thought. They were best friends from school days. An unlikely pairing considering tall, angular Emma's rich auburn hair with matching, down to earth, feisty temper and petite, blonde, Jansy's angelic appearance coupled with her vivacious nature. In the past Emma's impetuosity and caustic wit frequently landed them in trouble, while Jansy's sweet disposition beguilingly extricated them from many a tricky situation.

A broad smile spread across her face as she remembered some of the scrapes they'd got into and recalled how protective of his little sister Roger Cooper had been. Emma also knew, from hints dropped by Jansy, that in his teens Roger had been sweet on her but Emma found that hard to believe because he had persistently taunted her so. *Nevertheless, I am looking forward to seeing my old sparring partner once again,* and she grinned as the memories leaped into her mind.

Emma completed her present wrapping and approached the coming evening with keen anticipation. She enjoyed carol singing and looked forward to joining a crowd of friends from church as they sang their way around the village. It was such a special time, uniting villagers in a common focus, church goers and non-believers alike celebrating because of the birth of a baby.

Because of You, Lord, Emma reflected, *because of Your coming to earth as a baby, hearts are mellowed, lives are changed. Thankyou for the change You make in my life each day. When I look back, I can't believe how rude and awkward my behaviour was. How I fought against You and disobeyed You, yet You still loved me. Mum and Dad were so patient with me. How they prayed for my salvation. When I eventually acknowledged my sin and accepted Your forgiveness, the joy and peace in my heart was overwhelming.*

Emma wrapped her arms around herself, looked out of the window as the afternoon drew in, and through the twilight glimpsed flurries of snow wafting through the air, settling on all in its path. She picked out the stars shining brightly in the darkening sky and pondered on the star that shone over Bethlehem. For some moments she mulled over the mystery of that particular star; its ability to cause intelligent men to follow it to Bethlehem, leaving home, giving up everything, keenly focused, willing to be led.

Emma struggled with that concept. She still wanted her own way, she needed to be in control, she had her own agenda, her own goal, which was to be an art teacher and ultimately manage her own art gallery. She was willing to work hard to achieve that aim. The objective was almost in reach and to change direction was almost unthinkable; in fact, to her mind, impossible. *Impossible? With God nothing is impossible.*

Where had that thought sprung from? *Probably something Mum or Dad had once said.*

Emma shook herself. *Oh God, please don't ask me to change direction.* She turned from the bedroom window then concentrated on packing a bag in readiness for spending Christmas with her sister and family. Once ready, she checked again that all the doors in the shop were securely locked and left the flat eager to meet up with her friends at Alex's for carol singing.

As she stepped gingerly on the frozen ground, a police car passed her. She vaguely followed its progress along the road, and then glanced back at the Stores. Her father's instructions came to mind, *must remember to put the milk crate out in the morning.* She continued along the lane appreciating the intricate filigree patterns the frost was designing on the fences and hedging. As she neared the gate to Alex and Graeme's garden another police car drove silently by closely followed by an equally silent ambulance. *I wonder what's going on.*

Emma knocked at the Castleton's door, and admired the colourful, festive holly wreath Alex had hung above the knocker, as she entered. No sooner had she stepped inside than Bethany toddled across the hallway to greet her accompanied by Graeme.

"Emm, Emm," she called out with unreserved delight, putting her arms up to Emma who picked her up and swung her around in the air to the accompaniment of shrieks of enjoyment.

"Hello, little lady," Emma hugged her niece, kissed her cheek, then gently lowered her to the floor.

"It's good to see you, Em, come into the warm. Alex is in the kitchen putting finishing touches to our meal. Bethany and I are off to have fun in the bath," explained Graeme. The moment he mentioned the word "bath" Bethany pulled urgently on his hand as her little legs attempted to master the stairs.

Emma took off her coat and, as she hung it on the coat peg, smiled at the antics of her niece.

"There's a lot of police activity out there this evening. An ambulance passed me, too, as I approached your gate. I wonder if they've found Nicky."

"I don't know," Graeme replied thoughtfully, as he paused on the stairs, "but I also saw an ambulance and police car earlier this afternoon and Tom Catchpole and young Prettyman were scouting around on Sparham's Corner for a fair time, too. There certainly seems to be something going on."

"Should we ring Rosalie?"

"I'm not sure."

"Hello, Em," Alex wandered through from the kitchen and warmly greeted her sister. "Why do we need to ring Rosalie?" She looked up at Graeme.

"There seems to be an unusual amount of police and paramedic presence in the village and we were wondering as to the possible reason, Nicky being uppermost in our minds," Graeme explained.

"I think rather than speculate we ought to pray," commented Alex quietly, "knowing the village grapevine I'm sure we shall hear soon enough."

Oh, Miss Goody-Two-Shoes, always right as usual. Emma bristled.

"Splash, Dadda, splash," insisted Bethany tugging at her father's hand. Emma's brief crotchety moment passed as the adults laughed and Graeme and Bethany proceeded to the bathroom with haste and Alex tucked her arm through Emma's. "Come into the sitting room and rest your legs. You must be shattered after such a long, busy day."

Emma giggled. "To tell you the truth I fell asleep as soon as I got into the flat."

It was Alex's turn to chuckle. "I did the same when I got home. When I woke Graeme had given Bethany her tea and made a start on our meal. We then got involved in decorating the tree, setting out the Nativity scene and putting up a few trimmings. Bethany loved it. You should have seen her face when we turned on the tree lights. It just glowed with wonder.

She was quite fascinated with the woollen Nativity figures Aunt Bernice made for her. Look, we placed them on the coffee table so they would be in her line of vision but she can't resist the sheep and baby Jesus. They both fit snugly into her hand and she keeps picking them up and carrying them around with her and saying, "Baa, baa and babe Jees."'" There were shouts of glee and lots of giggles coming from the bathroom.

"It sounds as though the merriment is continuing," Emma nodded towards the open door as she fingered the tactile, child friendly Nativity figures.

"Yes, she is such fun to have around, a bundle of mischief, into everything now that she is independently mobile but, oh, such a joy," Alex beamed with contentment.

Emma looked into her sister's face, which evidenced such a depth of serenity, she felt she was trespassing on holy ground.

"You are very fortunate, Alex," she said, her voice thick with emotion.

"Yes, I am," Alex responded simply. "God has been good to us. I never dreamed life could be so rich and fulfilling. Graeme has strength and determination and takes his role as head of our family seriously, yet he is also gentle and loving. Fatherhood is precious to him and he willingly shares the load, nappy changing, as well as the fun times."

Alex rose to attend to their meal, and then she paused and looked thoughtfully at Emma.

"What are you going to do about Roger Cooper, Em?"

"Oh, I'll keep him at arm's length so his barbed remarks won't have opportunity to penetrate my armour," she replied glibly.

"Em, please don't pick a fight with him. It creates such an unpleasant atmosphere for everyone else."

"I pick a fight!" Emma shouted indignantly, jumping up and following Alex into the kitchen. "He is so self-righteous! He is always right! No one else's opinions carry any weight with him. It seems as if he can say what he likes and I have no right of reply."

"Em, please calm down," said Alex quietly, but firmly, as her sister slammed the cutlery on the table to add emphasis to her words.

"You both need to learn to listen to the other," Alex put her hand on Emma's arm. "Just a suggestion; when he says something that initially aggravates you, consciously count up to ten, or at least five," she amended quickly, knowing Emma's hasty temper, "before replying. Try it and see if it makes a difference."

"Oh, Alex you've no idea," Emma verbally exploded.

"I've always found him charming."

"He is infuriating! He deliberately goads me! Always comments on my hair and you know how that riles me."

"But, you have beautiful hair, Em."

"Humph!"

"Are you sure he's not trying to be complimentary?"

"Of course he's not! He's always referred to me as red-haired and fiery-tempered and the like."

"But that's in the past, surely…"

"Never, not with Roger! He delights in searching out new adjectives to equate my hair with my temper. I think the last were erubescent and irascible and we've already been through vinaceous and mercurial, rubricose and fervid as well as flame and peppery and the usual carrots and copper nut. This time will be no different."

"It can be, if you change your stance."

"Whatever do you mean?"

"Every time you meet you always expect to do battle with him so you prepare your defence or attack beforehand. For instance, you haven't seen one another for many months yet already you're thinking out your strategy for when you see him on Boxing Day."

"Of course I am!" confirmed Emma pumped up with indignation.

"Em, don't assume he'll be antagonistic. Smile while you count, then channel the conversation to a more neutral topic."

"But I need to be one step ahead of him before hostilities begin, that's why I make the necessary preparatory measures in advance. In fact only this afternoon I was actually looking forward to sparring with him."

"Oh, Em, he is right. You are irascible," Alex sighed. "You are both extremely likeable people; share Christian values yet your attitude is at variance with this viewpoint. Because your approach is negative you see Roger as bristly and objectionable and your hackles rise so that you never relax and enjoy one another's company. As I see it you purposely erect a confrontational barrier to protect your vulnerability."

"Alex, don't talk such nonsense," but Alex just shook her head despairingly.

"Do you want him to know the real Emma Kemp or just the fiery tempered red head you always present to him?"

"Of course," replied Emma reluctantly.

"Em, are you sure? Or are you fearful of him getting too close; fearful of the feelings that closeness ignites?"

Emma laughed. "Oh, Alex, aren't you being rather theatrical?"

Alex left the question unanswered, as she heard Graeme returning down the stairs, and prepared to serve their meal. However, Emma's heart, uncharacteristically for her, was thumping rapidly within her ribcage and her thoughts were in turmoil. She was so absorbed in trying to bring them into some semblance of order she barely heard Alex say, "God's grace is sufficient for every situation. Remember the Vicar's challenge? Why not pray for patience to cope with this awkward predicament? Never underestimate God's willingness to respond to your prayers, Em."

After tea there was a phone call from Val and Mick to say that they'd made good progress. Alex pressed the speaker button on the hand set so that they could all participate in the conversation.

"We've just run into a snow storm," Val explained.

"Where are you?" asked Emma.

"On the A1, just north of Morpeth, I think," replied Val.

"Are you alright?" enquired Alex.

"Yes, we're fine. We decided to have a break so we've pulled into a service station which typically has closed early because it's Christmas and also, I suspect, due to weather conditions to allow staff to get home safely."

"We're glad of the soup and sandwiches you made us take, Alex," shouted Mick.

"The snow doesn't seem to be settling too thickly at the moment, although visibility is somewhat murky, so we'll wait for the storm to pass before continuing our journey."

"Love to you all."

"Bye, take care. We're soon off carolling, but Graeme will be here, so ring and give us an update of your progress."

Well swathed, in order to combat the coldness of the night, Stephen Cooper set off to meet up with the rest of the carol singers at the home of Laura and Adam Catton. On the way he called at the Andaman's house as planned before Nicky's disappearance firstly, to learn if there was any news about his friend and secondly, to accompany Annette, if she felt she could cope with carolling in the circumstances.

He knocked on the back door and walked in, as was his custom, and was staggered speechless when he saw Nicky sitting in a chair by the kitchen table. In shock he stood rooted to the floor gaping at his friend taking in the grey, drawn features. In disbelief Stephen shook his head then, hesitatingly, he moved forwards his hand extended in greeting when he noticed a considerable gash on the side of Nicky's head, which had been shaved and stitched.

"How you doing, mate?"

Nicky looked up cautiously and acknowledged Stephen with a grimace.

"So, so," he replied gingerly rocking his raised right hand to and fro.

"It's great to see you. We've all been so worried about you." Though genuinely glad to see Nicky, Stephen was uncertain how to proceed, "Uhmm... what's er happened to er..." He broke off as the door swung open and Sergeant Catchpole came through to the kitchen.

"Aah, Stephen! Just the boy I be wanting."

"Oh?" Stephen looked questioningly at the Sergeant.

"Yes, m'boy. If we're to catch the blighters who did this to your pal we've got to have a plan and I think you be the best one to help us work out our strategy and put it into action. What dew yew say to that?"

Somewhat astonished at being taken into police confidence Stephen was lost for words but Tom Catchpole, who had given careful thought to his approach, called Annette to join him and the boys and said, "Now, this be what I want yew t'dew," and proceeded to acquaint them with relevant facts. Together they formulated a workable plan of action. To ensure a positive response to the operation he swore them to secrecy. This mantle did not fall serenely around Annette's shoulders who was more used to openness and honesty in her dealings with others. With gentle persuasion Tom convinced her to see the rightness of it in this situation if Nicky's attackers were to be brought to justice.

Shortly after their briefing, Annette and Stephen left the Andaman home to meet up with Miranda and Hilary Cooper, Josh Cook and Ryan Saunders; Jacqueline Cooper having gone to babysit Mark and Rhoda, in order to allow Ben and Rachel Durrant to join the carollers. On the way Stephen quizzed Annette about the details of Nicky's disappearance and injuries.

"Dave and Uncle Doug were preparing to dredge the harbour when they found Nicky unconscious, in the stern of the "Sunburst", covered with a tarpaulin," she explained. "Sergeant Catchpole thinks the movement Dave thought he saw, earlier in the day, is either linked to Nicky being put into the boat or someone checking up that he was still in situ."

"How did he get there?"

"No idea! Nicky can vaguely remember leaving your home last night but can't recall anything in between then and when he woke up in hospital this afternoon. They wanted to keep him in hospital for observation but as soon as his wounds were cleaned and stitched he was determined to come home."

"That sounds like Nicky."

"He seems to have lost a day along the way. He thought he still had the Stores deliveries to do. The rest you know. One thing really puzzles me. If it wasn't Nicky who came in the house last night, who was it?"

"That is a mystery. Obviously you were meant to believe Nicky was home."

"Well, someone went to extraordinary lengths to ensure we believed that."

"Mmm! It was important to someone that he was not reported missing last night. I don't think the perpetrator of this crime intended Nicky to be found, at least, not before Christmas."

"If that's the case something more sinister is implied." Annette paused for a moment, looked straight at Stephen and said slowly, "Does Nicky know something incriminating about someone that he's not aware of, which is so serious, he has to be silenced?"

"I don't know. I'm not aware of any strangers in the village therefore Nicky's assailant could well be someone we know. For that reason we're going to have to be on our guard."

"Watch what we say and not go out alone, you mean?"

"Yes, something like that."

"That's awful. We're going to view everyone, even friends, with suspicion and have misgivings about all their actions and motives."

Annette gasped and looked up at him in horror. "Whatever is someone so keen to hide?"

Stephen gently held her arm and smiled.

"I don't know. We've just got to be careful and watchful not melodramatic."

"And pray."

Stephen nodded. "And remember the police are acting on information they have received, of which, we are not aware."

Their discussion stopped as up ahead they could see his cousins, Miranda and Hilary, well wrapped up against the weather, step through their doorway. They greeted one another cheerfully but Hilary moved towards Annette warily.

"Hi, Annette, I'm surprised but glad to see you. Is there any news about Nicky?"

Annette felt uncomfortable, looked down at the ground and slowly shook her head. Stephen, sensing her discomfort, quickly changed the focus of their conversation and asked if they'd seen Josh and Ryan who were due to meet them by the bus stop opposite the girl's home.

"No, we've not seen them," replied Miranda, thinking Annette's response was out of concern for her missing brother.

"Oh, well, perhaps they've gone on. We are much later than we arranged," explained Stephen walking alongside them.

They soon arrived at Adam and Laura's house where the other carollers were chatting and enjoying the nibbles Laura had prepared. Stephen overheard someone mention a break-in at the Manor but Adam was keen to get underway so he was unable to question the speaker and learn anymore details.

"We've a number of request visits to make as well as the scheduled ones. If everyone's ready we'll call at the residential home in the Close first of all."

"Thanks for the eats, Laura, Happy Christmas."

Cheerful banter, fun and laughter between the young people provided momentum and kept up their spirits, despite the cold night air as they walked between each port of call. At about 8 o'clock Stephen knocked at Graeme and Alex's door as the carol singers passed by. Graeme had persuaded Alex to join Emma and the others so that he could wrap up her present.

"But you've had all day to do it," she laughed.

Graeme just grinned mischievously.

Whilst waiting for Alex and Emma to put on their coats the group sang, "Once in Royal David's City". Doors opened and neighbours listened or joined in as voices filled the air and the atmosphere throbbed with excitement. Emma's whole being tingled with joy.

"We intend to finish up at St. Andrews for carols by candlelight at a quarter past eleven, Graeme. We'll see Alex and Emma home just after midnight," called out Ben Durrant, "Happy Christmas."

Emma and Alex were mingling amongst their friends exchanging Christmas greetings when Miranda Durrant caught up with them.

"Hi, you two," she smiled at them both, "have you heard anything about this break-in at the Manor?"

Emma shook her head. "No, but the emergency services seem to have been busy in the village this afternoon."

"Oh?"

"An ambulance and two police cars passed me on my way to Alex's house, and Graeme also saw others earlier. We did wonder if it had anything to do with Nicky," she added quietly looking thoughtfully towards Annette.

"No news," murmured Miranda "so apparently not."

A snowball whizzed through the air and landed on Emma's shoulder. She looked up. Ryan and Josh were busily collecting more soft snow.

"C'mon slow coaches, yew'll never get in the heavenly choir if yew dawdle 'cus yew're mardling," Ryan called out cheekily throwing the ball he had moulded in his hands.

The girls laughed and quickened their paces, Alex somewhat reluctantly because of the unease she still felt over her earlier dealings with Josh. As they caught up with the boys her heart was heavy but Emma unaware of her sister's apprehension asked, "What's happened at the Manor?"

"Dunno," Ryan responded immediately. Alex watched Josh. Although unable to see his face clearly she sensed from his stance and manner he was uncomfortable. She decided to take the bull by the horns and asked, "How's Mrs Jenner, Josh?"

"Eh?"

"Mrs Jenner? She must have recovered quickly after you delivered her pension because she was in the shop at lunch time getting groceries."

Josh gulped.

"Number three on the carol sheet," Adam called out.

Reprieve, thought Josh and, gabbing Ryan's arm, distanced himself as far as he could from Alex and Emma as the joyful singing filled the cold night air. Alex was left staring into the darkness. The carol came to an end.

"Make it snappy. Keep together," Adam urged as the clusters of friends proceeded briskly to Green Pastures, the home of Roy and Bernice Durrant. Falling snow enhanced the picturesque Christmas card setting of the lovely house and despite frozen toes and fingers Emma was enraptured by the delightful scene, her artist's eye sweeping across the panoramic perspective lit up before her, as she walked up the driveway with Alex and Mirry.

"Wow! Just look at those lights."

"Must have cost a packet!"

"What a fairy-tale picture," were the comments around her but Emma saw the form of the trees, the shape of the shrubs silhouetted against the intriguing architecture of the old house in juxtaposition, wreathed in a night time blanket of snow, under a star spangled sky and Adam appropriately chose "In the Bleak Mid-Winter" to sing outside the front door. As their united voices rose harmoniously in song the door was flung open wide in greeting. Bernice stood there beaming, arms outstretched, as if to embrace them all in her welcome.

"Come in, come in you all," she graciously invited as the carol concluded.

The warmth of Bernice's hospitality was echoed by the roaring log fire Roy was busily stoking up. Its glow drew the carollers through the welcoming holly festooned hallway into the spacious sitting room. The heat gradually permeated their chilled extremities as they settled cosily in every available space on chairs and carpet around it.

"Move up, please, Gordon, make room for someone else to feel the fire," said Bernice to her brother-in-law, who was sprawled across the sofa.

"Don't see why I should," he muttered stroppily. "I'm comfortable. They chose to traipse out in the cold, I didn't. Letting in the frosty, wintry air, making us suffer. Selfish lot, inflicting their caterwauling on us, shouldn't be allowed," he complained loudly.

Bernice smiled around the room, "Everyone is a welcome guest, here."

"Some thinks they're more welcome than others, act like they've rights to other's property, snooping about, helping themselves. I've seen yew up to your trickery. Yew're phoney, the lot of yew but I'll catch yew one of these days. Christmas! Bah! A load of religious squit!" Gordon shouted angrily.

There was a stunned silence. The carollers looked at each other with questioning bewilderment. Ben moved quickly to sit by his father and spoke with him quietly. His calm manner diffused the awkward situation Gordon's quarrelsome mood had created so that his intention to spoil the evening was thwarted.

At the same time Roy touched his son, Justin's arm, nodded to Adam and smiled at his niece, Annelie. Almost imperceptibly Adam's conducting hand beat a rhythm, and as one, voices joined together in a harmonious humming accompaniment, as Justin and Annelie delighted everyone with their vocal duet rendering of "O Holy Night". Everyone, that is, except Gordon whose response to his daughter's singing was scathing. Bernice disregarded Gordon's sarcastic comments, held both Annelie's hands in her own, "Well done, my dear, that was such a blessing." Spontaneous applause resounded in approval around the room.

All too soon it was time to leave the cosy warmth of Green Pastures and move on to the next port-of-call.

Quite a number of people were huddled around the front door at Pauline and Billy Cooper's house as the carol singers processed, with lanterns aloft, to join them. The falling snow was settling and the north easterly wind was biting.

"Shall we sing, "See amid the winter's snow", Adam?" someone called out.

"Yes, why not? Number 25 everybody."

As voices rang out in the cold night air, Miranda opened the front door, "We're here," she called but was puzzled by the lack of response. She kicked off her boots and walked through to the kitchen. Lights were on throughout the house and the aroma emanating from the kitchen suggested food was heating in the oven but there was no sign of either of her parents. The other young folk followed her in. She took the trays of food out of the oven and set them on mats on the table, then searched across the sea of faces for Hilary. She spotted her and swiftly reached her side, grabbed her sister's arm and whispered, "Hills, Mum and Dad don't seem to be here. I'm going to phone their mobiles. Get the gang to help you serve the eats and pour the coffee. I won't be long." Before Miranda could lift the house phone, it rang.

"Hello."

"Mirry?"

"Oh, Dad, is everything OK? I was so worried."

"I've left you a note on the dining room table."

"We're in the kitchen."

Her father laughed. "Trust you to follow your nose."

"Where are you?"

"The vicarage. The Vicar's wife has had an accident."

"Oh dear, how is she?"

"Not too good. The paramedics have taken Mrs Darnell to hospital."

"What about the children and where's the Vicar?"

"We're sitting in with Ellie and Gareth so that the Rev Hugh can be with his wife."

"Mum must be shattered. She was up so early this morning. I'll come over straight away and relieve her. Hilary's in her element organizing everyone here."

"That's good of you Mirry. I'd like to speak to Ben if he's there."

"OK, I'll just get him."

Miranda made her way back to the kitchen where there was a happy hubbub of noise.

"I say everyone," she called clapping her hands to catch attention.

"Sh! Sh!"

"Mrs Darnell's had an accident. I don't know any details. Ben, Dad wants a word."

Alex shuddered at the news. "Dear Lord, what is happening, today?" she murmured.

"Adam, we must pray," urged Annette to the subdued company.

"You're right, Justin will you lead us?"

Ben crept from the prayerful hush in the kitchen to speak, on the phone in the hallway, with Billy Cooper. He was shocked to learn of the brutal attack on Penny Darnell but as Church deacons they sensitively made contingency plans to cover the remaining Christmas services for Hugh Darnell should it prove necessary.

CHAPTER SIX

See our numbers how they swell, thought Emma, sometime later, as quite a crowd trudged their way to Doctor Cooper's house. Underfoot it was getting slippery and quite treacherous but no one complained. It seemed that the sense of occasion kept up their spirits.

However, as Emma looked around the sea of faces lit up by the glow of the lanterns, her eye alighted on Tom Catchpole. In an anorak, with a woollen hat pulled down over his ears, he was hovering on the edge of the group, between Billy Knights and Josh Cook. *I wonder what he's doing here and so obviously incognito.* Whilst still watching him she saw him give an almost imperceptible nod. She followed the line of his gaze. It stopped at Stephen Cooper who blinked in acknowledgement, then announced in a loud voice, "I'll just phone Mum to say we're on the way so that she can have soup ready for our arrival."

"Brill, mate," enthused Ryan thumping Stephen playfully on the shoulder.

"Yeah, it's freezing now," grumbled Josh gruffly, briskly stamping his feet on the ground.

Others greeted this news with applause and cheers as they, too, were feeling quite cold, blowing on hands, or repeatedly beating arms across chests, in an attempt to keep warm.

Crossing the Green it became evident the blizzard was getting heavier, since snowdrifts were accumulating, making walking more difficult. Nevertheless, with their lanterns held high, the snow-robed carollers still stopped outside to sing, "Hark the Herald Angels sing." Neighbours looked out of their windows enchanted by the sound and the scene. Some even braved the raw weather and joined their voices with those of the carol singers outside Doctor Cooper's house for the "Calypso Carol" and "Silent Night."

Emma, despite the chilliness, sang with abandon, along with the others, the modern as well as the traditional carols but stopped in full flow when she saw Roger Cooper leaning against the wall of the porch of his parent's home, his brown eyes, warm and twinkling focussed upon her. He held her gaze, grinned impishly, and mouthed across the distance between them, "Happy Christmas, Carrots."

Standing next to her Alex witnessed the exchange. She saw Emma tense and stiffen and sought to diffuse the situation promptly. "Em, take a deep breath," she whispered, "and smile." Remembering her sister's earlier advice Emma complied, not realising how delightful her smiling face appeared to Roger, causing his heart to somersault in an unaccustomed fashion. The antagonistic feelings Emma anticipated did not emerge. The conscious effort to respond to Roger positively left her glowing with unimaginable, favourable vibes. Grabbing Alex's arm she said excitedly, "It works." Alex smiled and inwardly prayed, *Thankyou, Lord.*

"Hi, Roger, home for Christmas?"

"Good to see you, pal."

"How yew doin' mate?"

Hearty greetings, extended hands, pats on the back cascaded around him, as Roger struggled against the flow making its way into his parent's home, intent on reaching Emma's side anxious to commence Christmas celebrations with her in a cordial, unruffled manner.

Lord, help me to be patient where Emma is concerned. Teach me Your will and show me Your timing. If she is the one You have chosen for me reveal it also to her.

The surge of bodies, anxious for warmth, halted abruptly, hindering his progress. Then, audible gasps prompted him to glance up. The stunned expression on Emma and Alex's faces perplexed Roger so he turned round to see what had caused their look of horror.

Through the doorway walked Josh Cook, escorted by Sergeant Catchpole and handcuffed to P.C. Prettyman, closely followed by his own father, Doctor John. He was supporting a sickly looking Nicky Andaman accompanied by Annette and his brother, Stephen. On the road Roger could see the blue flashing lights of a police car flanked by a stationary 4X4 with Melvin Andaman behind the wheel. *What's going on?* He looked enquiringly in Emma's direction especially when Tom Catchpole stopped and said quite distinctly to Alex and Emma, "I'll need to have a word with you two, later."

Adam, anxious to lift the mood, re-establish the focus and channel the caroller's attention started to sing, "Away in a manger." One by one, voices blended together. Automatically they linked arms, making a united body as they sang.

"Be near me, Lord Jesus...close...for ever...I pray...Bless all the dear children in Thy tender care..."

Because of You, Lord Jesus, we can pray for one another. Thankyou that Nicky has been found and is alive, prayed Alex silently. *I don't understand what is happening today but keep all in Your loving care.*

At the conclusion of the carol a very subdued group passed through the hallway of the Doctor's house helping themselves to the welcome cups of warming soup that Trixie had so thoughtfully prepared.

"Make your way into the conservatory, please," she called, "then there will be sufficient room for everyone."

As the crowd warmed through, conversation naturally became animated, and centred on what they had just witnessed.

"Didn't Nicky look ghastly?"

"Wonder what happened to him?"

"Missing all night, I hear."

"It seems as though he's taken a bit of a beating."

"You don't think Josh had anything to do with that?"

"'Course not, they're the best of friends."

"Then why the handcuffs and police escort?"

"Looks like he's tarred with the same brush as his Dad," said Billy Knights spitefully. "What dew yew say, Ryan."

"Doan't say that," replied Ryan glumly "he's a good mate."

"Yup, that's an unfair assumption, Billy. Josh is quite a nice boy underneath all that brashness. Probably acts like that to cover up how he feels about his Dad's behaviour since he was made redundant."

"Could be," commented someone thoughtfully. "I hear Joe's been taken into custody today."

"Oh no, not again! Poor Michelle, I think she's had a tough time dealing with those youngsters since Joe lost his job."

"Anyway, what yew doin' 'ere, Billy? Doan't usually see yew at church do's."

"Oh, I just thought I'd tag along as I'm ashore, it bein' Christmas."

"It's good to have you here."

Roger edged his way around the chatting friends towards where Emma was standing but the precise moment he managed to reach her side his father returned and asked for everyone's attention.

"Dear friends, I can't say too much about the matter so recently observed by us all because it is a police judiciary matter but, rather than fuel unhealthy speculation, I have Sgt Tom's permission to tell you that the incidents that have occurred in the village, during the past twenty-four hours, appear to be linked. Please do not discuss things between yourselves because he needs to interview many of you and wants first-hand accounts, not what you've heard or surmised from someone else. I trust you all to uphold his request."

Murmuring throughout the room indicated assent to this news.

"Doctor John, can we pray?" asked Annette tentatively as she too slipped back into the room having seen her brother safely home.

"Yes, many families in our community will be hurting this Christmas for different reasons and stand in need of our prayerful support as well as the reassurance of our Heavenly Father's loving presence."

Alex's heart churned within her and she clasped her sister's arm tightly. "Em, I think we've unwittingly become embroiled in the happenings of today."

Emma looked at her sister, startled. "Whatever do you mean? Don't talk nonsense," She tossed her auburn mane with annoyance.

Alex shook her head. "As Doctor John has said we really can't discuss it in case we influence one another's evidence but we are going to have to think very carefully about all the events that have taken place at the Stores today, the people who've been in, or not, what they have or have not said," she gently chided.

"I don't know what you're talking about. It's been a rather busy day and now you're tired and emotional," Emma retorted dismissively.

"Just give it some careful thought, Em. What you know will piece together like a jigsaw with what I know," responded Alex calmly.

Roger nodded in agreement and said softly, "With your artistic flair you have the ability to notice important details, Emma."

She peered at him quizzically. Was this a compliment or was he being sarcastic? It was on the tip of her tongue to take exception to his words and answer back with a barbed quip, but Alex intervened.

"When we're less tired and the situation not so traumatically charged we might recall more clearly our observations of today and be able to comment on things we heard or noticed."

"Good idea, Alex. I'm not sure what I've returned home to but the police seem to have it all under control. I really came over to wish you a Happy Christmas and say how good it is to see you both again." Roger looked directly at Emma as he spoke. She could hear the genuine warmth in his voice but was reluctant to accept it at face value. Very cautiously she glanced up at him expecting to see a roguish glint in his eye and quirky grin around his mouth. Instead, to her amazement, she saw a sincere smiling face overflowing with friendly affection. This conduct puzzled her. It was not how she had come to expect Roger Cooper to behave.

Her thoughts and emotions were in turmoil and she was glad of the soup Mrs Cooper thrust into her numbed hands. "Thankyou," she breathed, gratefully, and then concentrated on sipping the warming liquid, thus preventing further spoken communication with Roger, but he remained by her side, silent yet attentive. This totally unnerved her. She began to yearn for the good old days when the sparks would fly and they verbally sparred with one another, their caustic barbs cutting the air. At least that was familiar territory. Emma found this new approach from Roger difficult to handle. Slowly sipping the soup her thoughts raced away. Had he changed or was it she who was different? What had Alex said? Breathe deeply, count before speaking, smile and pray. It all came back to her. Her heart seemed to be thumping so wildly and loudly the whole room must be able to hear it. *Lord, I am so confused. Please give me peace and direction.*

His mind still reeling from the shock of discovering Nicky in the stern of his boat Dave drove thoughtfully to Norwich. Over and over he castigated himself for not checking more closely earlier in the day when he thought he had seen movement on the quay; Nicky could have been found sooner. The timing of Nicky's transfer to the "Sunburst" by his assailants baffled him, as did his cousin's whereabouts up to that point. Tom Catchpole had mentioned to Dave his keenness to establish this fact which is why he was avidly questioning everybody from the village.

"If you saw movement this morning, no matter how small, then so did someone else."

Dave was due to meet Jansy when she came off duty at 8 o'clock but the joy and excitement with which he had anticipated their meeting was now tempered with anxiety concerning his young cousin. Thankfully, he was found, and alive. Annette had rung from the hospital to say Nicky had recovered consciousness and, though somewhat hazy about what had happened to him, once his wounds had been attended to he insisted on being taken home. Like many, when they heard about his experience, Dave was perplexed over such a mindless attack. He was also concerned about the deliberate attempt to cover up the matter by the use of his boat which was now regarded as a scene of crime. As the events of the day tumbled about in his mind a prayer came from his heart.

Father God, what a topsy-turvy state this affair has brought to our community. I don't understand what is going on, but Father, I'm reminded that this is Your world; You are Lord, sovereign, and in control. Your children make choices which sometimes conflict with Your will, causing hurt and heartache. Father, I bring to You all those involved or touched in some way by this incident. All are known to You, if not to me. I trust You, Father, for their sakes. Help me now to focus on the darling girl You have given me. This is a special evening for us Father, envelope us in Your love and seal our commitment to each other and to You.

Approaching the city centre, traffic was building up and driving required all of his concentration, particularly as snow was beginning to fall more heavily. Nevertheless, he arrived at the hospital with time to spare and found a parking space in full view of the exit through which he expected Jansy to come. He turned off the ignition and breathed deeply, *Oh Lord, thankyou for Your constant presence.* From this vantage point he was able to watch for Jansy's arrival so welcomed these calming moments with his Lord.

Sometime later that evening, Jansy and Dave walked hand in hand, deep in conversation, oblivious to the rapidly falling snow. They had just shared an emotionally charged couple of hours and were returning to the car from one of their favourite restaurants.

"It was always expected that we would marry when we grew up; something that would happen in the future. I can't believe it's really happening now," said Jansy, her face radiant with wonder.

Dave drew closer to her, took her hand and gently squeezed it. "You can believe it, darling Jansy. I love you with all my heart now and for always. You're not having doubts are you?"

"Of course not," Jansy shook her blond head and smiled warmly up into the kind rugged face she knew almost as well as she knew her own. "It's just that now it's here it feels as though it's galloped up on us so fast."

"Jansy Cooper, I don't call seventeen years very fast, but I know what you mean. Very soon you'll be Mrs David Ransome. How will you like that?" Dave asked, still holding her hand. As they trod gingerly on the snow covered path, he turned to face her, smiling directly into her bright blue eyes.

"I'll let you know in another seventeen years' time. How will you like being the husband of Doctor Cooper's pretty daughter?" she grinned mischievously and swung his arm playfully.

"Uhm! I hadn't thought of that," Dave mused.

"Well, I've had a lifetime to get used to it. It comes with the territory."

They slowed and stopped automatically as they reached the river bank. Standing side by side they gazed through the falling snow at the dancing reflections, Christmas lights dangling from the riverside properties, made on the water. Dave put his arm around Jansy's shoulders.

"Let me tell you, my darling girl, it's you, Jansy Marcia Cooper, whom I love, wish to marry and spend the rest of my life with, not Doctor Cooper's daughter no matter how pretty she may be."

It was Jansy's turn to laugh. "That's a contradiction in terms. I'll always be the Doctor's daughter. That is a fact of history, recorded on my birth certificate. Can't get away from it; unless we go to deepest Africa where no one's ever heard of us."

"Life will never be dull with you, Jansy."

"Oh?" She inclined her head towards him, her eyes watching him questioningly, her chin raised, her pert little nose almost touching his cheek, her rosebud mouth inviting a kiss.

"Being together is going to be such a joy, Jansy. You've got this wonderful ability to see the best in everyone and the brightest side to everything but I never know what you're going to say next."

"Well, Mr Solemn-sides," she said, giggling and digging him in the ribs, "after your performance tonight it seems I, too, must be prepared for excitement and the unexpected around every corner."

"You didn't mind?"

"I thought the whole evening was delightful and such a surprise. You'd planned so meticulously and Guido, and his staff, entered into the spirit of things admirably."

"Well, of course, Guido's a romantic at heart. He was disappointed when I requested a very simple menu and put a time restraint on proceedings but his face was wreathed in smiles when I said we'd be back to sample one of his more exotic dishes another time."

"Yes, everything was just as I like it. Thankyou, my dearest, Dave, I couldn't have coped with anything too heavy or spicy this late in the evening but the melon, with raspberry coulis, was refreshing, the omelette, light and fluffy, and the Brule, simply divine. The three wise men as waiters were ingenious. Whose idea was that?"

"Oh, it evolved as we were planning the evening."

"How long ago was that?" asked Jansy impishly, thinking Dave had probably called Guido last time he was ashore.

"Last September."

"Oh, Dave," sighed Jansy dreamily, "I do love you."

"So, you enjoyed the Ransome revised standard version of Gold, Frankincense and Myrrh?" he asked with a chuckle in his voice.

"Dave, that was brilliant."

"Mmm, I thought so, too."

They'd quickened their paces, the force of the wind catching their breath, small particles of snow clinging to their clothing and freezing their extremities, glad to shake themselves and slip into the protection of the car. Jansy snuggled herself into the passenger seat and with arms wrapped around herself let out a sigh of contentment.

"Happy?" enquired Dave sliding into the driver's seat beside her.

"Mmm! Blissfully!"

As they left the city behind they sat in companionable silence while Dave concentrated on negotiating the increasingly treacherous roads.

He didn't want to spoil the euphoria of the evening for Jansy but he knew he should prepare her for the shocking scenario they would encounter when they reached the village. With eyes fixed on the road, his heart prayed for guidance and sensitivity in this matter.

"Busy day?"

"Yes," and he listened attentively as Jansy went on to elaborate different incidents that had occurred during her shift.

"How about you?"

In between recalling his early morning arrival in the harbour and leaving the village to meet her, he was able, in a matter of fact way, so as not to alarm her, to intersperse the day's events in the village with snippets about the circumstances concerning Nicky. He was unaware of the attack on Penny Darnell or the Manor House break-in or the arrest of Josh Cook, having left Newton Westerby before these events had become general knowledge. This being so, little did they appreciate that memory of this day would impact on the village in a fragmentary fashion; their engagement being just one segment of a shattered whole.

When Dave and Jansy arrived at the Cooper residence the windows blazed with light. Jansy estimated that all the rooms would be crammed with carollers. However, through the kitchen window she caught sight of her mother, apparently alone so, hand in hand, they crept in through the back door.

"Hi, Mum."

"Hello, you two. How are you?" said Trixie turning from her task, a warm smile of welcome on her face.

"Cold but happy…we've just got engaged."

"Oh, my dears, congratulations!"

"Where's Dad?"

"In the hall."

Jansy let go of Dave's hand and smiled at him encouragingly as he went to approach his future father-in-law. She closed the door behind him and leant back against it.

"Oh, Mum, it was so romantic. Dave met me from work and we went to La Rosa for a meal. Guido greeted us at the door and led us to a secluded table. As soon as we were seated and he'd arranged for our coats to be taken we were offered fruit punch. Then a peaceful hush came over the whole restaurant, it had been very noisy and boisterous as we arrived, and I could hear the strains of "O Holy Night." Mum, I can hardly describe it. It was awesome. I can understand how Moses felt standing in front of the burning bush when he sensed the presence of God and felt he was standing on hallowed ground. He took off his sandals. I just closed my eyes. The music stopped after the first verse. I opened my eyes and standing by our table was a wise man holding a velvet cushion on which was laid a single red rose. In one movement Dave got up, took the rose, and knelt on one knee by the side of me. He took my hand and offered me the rose as he said, "Jansy, I love you, will you be my wife?""

"Well, my dear," said Trixie, holding her daughter close to her, "I always looked upon Dave as solid, dependable, hardworking, sincere, warm and affectionate, a dear godly man, but never could I imagine him as an impetuous, romantic lover. However did you respond?"

"In the affirmative, of course," replied Jansy, her blue eyes dancing, her rosebud mouth stretching in a dreamy smile.

"After the refreshing starter it all happened again, verse two of "O Holy Night," another wise man and a gift of perfume. We enjoyed a delicious omelette then the third wise man bore aloft a small box to the accompaniment of a third verse. Dave took it and opened it. Just look, Mum." She held out her left hand wearing a diamond solitaire on her third finger.

"It's lovely, Jansy. I'm so pleased for you and I pray that you'll both be very happy." Trixie placed her hands gently on the shoulders of this, her only daughter, and tenderly kissed her cheek.

"You've both waited and worked hard for this day. I admire the manner in which you have conducted yourselves and prepared to embark on this very sacred relationship. God bless you and Dave." Trixie took out her hankie and blew her nose.

"Now, I think we ought to join the others."

She linked her arm through Jansy's and turned to go into the hallway when her husband, accompanied by Dave, came to join them. Doctor John embraced them both and leaned down to kiss Jansy's cheek. "I hear congratulations are in order, my dear. I pray the blessing and hope of our Lord upon you both. May His grace continue working in your lives and fill you with joy." Then he reached round to encompass Dave, his blue eyes twinkling and his mouth curved in mirth. "Good news is best shared; shall we?" Jansy and Dave looked at one another and replied, "Yes."

Knowing that they were as yet unaware of all that had taken place in the village during the day, Doctor John made the announcement of their engagement carefully, with warmth and sensitivity. As good wishes were showered upon the couple he suggested those of the assembled company wishing to attend the candle-lit service should make their way now or they might be too late.

The mood that had prevailed since Josh Cook's arrest lifted as the carollers flocked to congratulate Dave and Jansy and the elation of the moment carried them on their way across the Green to the Church.

As John and Trixie stood in the hallway bidding farewell to the stragglers the phone rang. The Doctor answered it. Only his nephew, Justin, of those still milling around, noticed the change in his countenance.

"Is everything OK?" he asked the Doctor.

With pursed lips John nodded and made his way to Trixie's side.

"I've changed my mind about the candle-lit service. I'll wander across with the youngsters, my love. I'll try not to be too late back."

Trixie looked closely at her husband, surprised and raised her eyebrows, knowing how adamant John had been about "not too late a night." He leaned forward to kiss her cheek and whispered, "Hugh's had a call about an accident and needs me."

"Penny?"

"No, someone else."

She put down the tray she was carrying. "I'll come with you. Give me a moment, I'll grab my coat," she smiled at him.

"That will be nice," John nodded at her, acknowledging the understanding she was giving, showing that she knew he needed her with him.

Arm in arm they followed the carol singers across the snow-carpeted Green. Ahead they saw Dave and Jansy sharing with Emma and Alex, accompanied by Justin and Miranda.

"Those two are going to need our love and prayers," John commented quietly.

At that moment they were joined by other Church goers so Trixie was unable to ask which two he meant. She was to remain in the dark for quite some time and was deeply troubled as to whom John was referring and what had happened.

CHAPTER SEVEN

"Love came down at Christmas." Hugh looked down at his congregation, bathed in candle light, with compassion. After the horrific events in the village he'd felt compelled to change the message he had prepared earlier. His people were hurting and he was hurting with them; his own wife being one of the subjects of attack. He also had the burdensome knowledge of the greater pain some of his parishioners were going to suffer, when news he had received broke, after the service ended.

"Love came down at Christmas," he repeated. "I think some of us are struggling with that concept at the moment. Our feelings are reflecting many emotions after our experiences today and love is not uppermost on our agenda. How many of you are straining to allow love a foothold right now? It's hard, isn't it?

"But this is Christmas! Just as two thousand years ago, so today, the Word of God assures us that Love, in the form of Jesus Christ, exchanged the splendour of heaven for the sordid realm of earth, for us. What a contrast! He was used to basking in the glory of God, accepting worship and adoration from the angels. He stepped down from the beauty and perfection surrounding His Father's throne to the bare rudimentary provision of a stable in an inhospitable world which had no room for him. That same Love, incarnate in Jesus Christ, is still willing to enter our hostile environment but hearts are closed to Him, unwilling to accept the free gift of redemption which is offered to them. Self, greed, bitterness or indifference are barriers, at the heart of our society today, to the divine work of love and grace.

"Love came down at Christmas. Love reaches out to each of us; don't shut Him out. We need love to cope with our pain. Our Father, God, knows and understands. At His moment of intense suffering Jesus recognised this, too. His response was to pray, "Father, forgive.""

"May I suggest that you each allow His love to, not only envelope you, but also to indwell you, enabling you to echo our Lord's words, "Father, forgive." I believe this is the only way we can cope with the heartache we share this Christmas.

"Love never fails. The psalmist proved the pricelessness of the unfailing love of God to be true and if we want to know the joy of that experience we are going to have to trust that same God who excels in turning mourning into dancing and sorrow into joy. It isn't adorned with brightly coloured wrapping paper decorated with pretty bows and tinsel. It's a gift that comes without embellishments. He tells us clearly what it is in John 10 v 10, "I have come that you may have life." This is my gift to you. Life with Love. Please accept it.""

Hugh sat down. An awesome hush pervaded the Church.

Ben stood. In his position as lay reader he had led the early part of the service until Hugh had returned from the hospital with Penny, now, as he announced the final carol and invitation to the vicarage for refreshments, there were murmurings amongst the congregation. Some silently applauded the Vicar's courage for tackling issues that were bothering so many of them. Others, not entirely au fait with the day's incidents and their consequences, were surprised at his forthrightness. The effort had drained him. It did not go unnoticed.

"Just look at the strain etched upon his face," whispered Trixie to John.

"His heart must be breaking to think that someone in the parish should so viciously violate his precious wife and be the perpetrator of other atrocities to fellow citizens of the village," replied the Doctor.

"John!" admonished Trixie quietly. "Are you judge and jury?"

"No, more's the pity. If I were on the bench they'd be hung, drawn and quartered for what they have done today."

"You know who THEY are, do you?"

"I've a fair idea, my dear. But you know the law; innocent till proven guilty." He put his arm affectionately around her shoulders. "Now, let's make our way to the vicarage. We're going to be needed there."

They smiled as the chattering young people, clustered around Dave and Jansy, passed them. They also acknowledged the warm wishes of fellow worshippers as they exited the Church.

At the door they shook hands with Ben and the Vicar.

"Well done, young man. Considering you stepped in at short notice you conducted the service admirably, with deep feeling and sensibility, Ben. Rather difficult to create an atmosphere of joy amid such a plethora of emotion."

"Thankyou, Doctor."

"Not at all, Ben. We're indebted to you and your willingness to pilot things through for us. Have a good Christmas with your family, especially now that Nicky is found. Good night."

"God bless you Doctor; Mrs Cooper."

John and Trixie inclined their heads in acknowledgement and made to move on.

"John," the Vicar called.

The Doctor turned and placed a firm hand on Hugh's shoulder. "See you shortly, Hugh." The Vicar looked at him grimly and nodded.

Outside the Church they bumped into a small group who were trying to persuade Alex to stay for refreshments.

"I really would like to go home," she said.

"Why not come over to the vicarage for five minutes just to see Jansy, admire her ring and congratulate her and Dave on their engagement? You know, make it special for them. It must be terribly deflating for them to come home to such horridness," said Emma pressingly. When she saw the Doctor and Mrs Cooper she enlisted their help. "Doctor John, please persuade Alex to stay for a short time."

"Look, my dears, why don't you step inside briefly, sample the delicious refreshments Penny prepared before her accident then I'll happily escort you home," said John persuasively.

"Doctor, you don't have to go to all that trouble. We..." began Alex but Roger butted in, "Dad, I'll walk up the lane with Emma and Alex, save you trundling all that way and back in this weather."

"I'm not in my dotage yet, my man, but I am feeling the cold so let's get indoors."

The young people followed his lead and made their way towards the vicarage. Emma found she was plodding through the snow next to John so she asked, "Doc, do you know what happened to Mrs Darnell?"

"I don't know all the details, Emma, but I think it best if I don't discuss what I do know as fact till Sgt Catchpole has had opportunity to interview us all."

Emma nodded, "I understand, but is she home?"

"Yes, I believe so."

"I'm glad for Ellie and Gareth's sake. It wouldn't be a pleasant Christmas for them if their Mum was in hospital. It's a special time for families to get together, isn't it? I think we'll find it odd tomorrow not having Mum and Dad spending the day with us. I don't begrudge them a break or opportunity to have time with Drew and Morag but it will be the first time we haven't had them around at Christmas."

John's heart bled for this lovely young woman by his side. However, the moving throng ensured they were separated and John was spared from replying. A pungent aroma from mulled spices and fruit greeted their arrival at the vicarage door as the surge of other guests swept them inside. Surprisingly, there were quite a number of people milling around in the vicarage hallway and kitchen, despite the diminished attendance at the service because of the deteriorating weather conditions. John looked round for Trixie, his height enabling him to see clearly across most of the heads gathered there. Sighting her coming through the sitting room door he hurriedly reached her side.

"Checking on Penny?"

"Mmm, rather battered and bruised but settled and comfortable," she replied quietly.

"Typical medical-speak," John said with a forced smile.

"That's living with you for so long," Trixie retorted with a shrug. He put a hand under her elbow and guided her to the Vicar's study. Hugh Darnell, still attired in his outer garments, was seated at his desk, his head in his hands, his eyes closed in prayer. As the door clicked he looked up and turned to John and Trixie. Getting up and making his way towards them with outstretched hands he said, "Thankyou for your support. I suggest we leave the door open and let the youngsters spill over into here. I think the girls will need to be surrounded by their friends."

"What...?" began Trixie, and then faltered.

Hugh reached out and took hold of her hands. He looked directly at her. "I'll come straight to the point; Mick and Val have been killed in a road accident on their way to Edinburgh. Inspector Capps has had calls from Northumbrian police. I understand they're viewing the circumstances as suspicious despite the atrocious weather conditions."

Trixie gasped in strangled anguish, "Oh, dear Lord, whatever else is going to happen today? Those poor girls!"

John put his arm tenderly around her. "You OK?"

She nodded; blew her nose and wiped her eyes. Giving his wife a moment to compose herself, John assisted Hugh with his overcoat then, opened the study door wide. He spoke to one or two people as he made his way to the kitchen where Miranda Durrant was skilfully organizing everyone with mince pies and drinks. Admiring her skill he thought, No *wonder my waiting room runs like clockwork.* Miranda was his receptionist. *Good choice,* he nodded to himself. As he was usually in the surgery when she was working he had never before seen her in full flow.

John picked up a couple of drinks for Trixie and Hugh, then, elbowed his way back to the study, deftly avoiding any spillages. He was pleased to see a number of people had trickled into the study, Alex and Emma amongst them. He distributed the drinks then turned back to the group the girls were with. He put his arms around their shoulders and said quietly, "Girls, the Vicar has some bad news to share with you."

Alex looked up at him in alarm and he felt Emma stiffen beneath his touch.

"Bethany?"

"Mum and Dad?" they asked simultaneously.

"Come and sit down."

A deathly hush fell on the group immediately surrounding the sisters as they parted to allow them through to the armchairs.

"Alex, Emma, there is no easy way to tell you this. I wish to God there were. Your Mum and Dad have died in a road accident."

Emma jumped up indignantly, "Don't be silly. It can't possibly be. It's a mistake," she declared emphatically. "We spoke to them just before we left home to come carol singing. There were only flurries of snow and they were waiting till it eased. You're wrong. It's a mistake!" Her voice crescendoed and she stomped about the study in disbelief at the news she had just received. She gesticulated wildly to those next to her. "NO! NO! NO! It's NOT true," she screamed. Unwilling to accept Hugh's words she pushed her hands through her hair and distraughtly pulled at the roots and frenziedly stamped her feet.

Although shocked by the news, Jansy stayed close to Emma, whilst Dave slipped out of the study and quietly passed on the sad news to those in the hall and kitchen. Stunned, the groups of people stopped conversing and prayed for Alex and Emma and the wider family; a number of those present were related in some way, cousins or nephews and nieces to Val and Mick. Then, in hushed tones they spoke of their Christian witness at Church, through the Village Stores and in the village community. Alex's faith was strengthened and encouraged by the pockets of prayerful support of believers around her but Emma's heart was hardened.

"This is Christmas Eve; they rang, they were OK. Mum said so. It's not true!" Emma continued to rant. She stopped in front of John Cooper and beat him repeatedly upon the chest, "You knew! You knew!" she shouted accusingly, "and you didn't say anything. You let me go on about missing them without stopping me."

"Emma, Emma," called Alex softly, "it is true. The Vicar would not lie to us," her voice broke and she sobbed quietly. Trixie sat on the arm of the chair and held her gently, speaking soothing words of comfort and praying that both Alex and Emma, in the pain of their loss, would know the presence of the One who so wonderfully comforts and strengthens. Her caring heart and cradling arms did much to bring peace and calm to Alex's troubled soul. In those quiet moments the realisation came to her, "They're spending Christmas in the presence of the Lord," she murmured.

Hugh, who was standing close by, overheard. He nodded and said, "Yes, I believe they are, even now, enjoying the splendours of heaven." Emma, from her position at the edge of the group heard his words and remarked bitterly, "You said they were dead. Dead! How can they enjoy anything? How can any of us enjoy anything ever again?"

Hugh turned towards her and said gently, "Emma, I'm truly sorry about what has happened to your Mum and Dad. I understand that right now it is difficult to take in. You're hurting but we have a God who is able to comfort, strengthen and sustain us in our times of pain. He loves you."

"Don't talk to me about God," she retorted angrily. "How can He care if He lets this happen? This Christian stuff; it's rubbish if this is what He allows. Mum and Dad never hurt anyone. Why them? Why not evil people who'd deserve it?"

"Emma," said Roger Cooper kindly but firmly, aware that she was allowing her feelings to impair her judgement. He was anxious that she didn't say anything more in her distressed state that she might later regret. This dear, young woman, who was so special to him, was hurting and there was nothing he could do to alleviate her pain except pray and be there for her. At the moment she didn't want him, or anyone else, and was lashing out indiscriminately because of her wretchedness.

"I'll walk you home."

She looked at him thunderously but before she could reply, Alex stood and calmly said, "Thankyou, Roger. We'll go home now, Emma." She put her arm through her sister's, bidding goodnight to friends who were still praying for them, and steered Emma towards the door. In her own heart she voiced a prayer, *Father God, thankyou for these kindly folk who are loving and supporting us in Your name,* which rose in gratitude from her heart as she left the Vicar's study. The Cooper family, along with Dave, surrounded Alex and Emma to accompany them on their inhospitable journey home.

"Graeme?" Alex enquired of John as they walked along the hallway.

"Hugh went to see him as soon as he got the call. He didn't know you were out with the carollers. Graeme suggested waiting until after the service to tell you. Sgt Catchpole has been to tell Roy and Bernice, Gordon and Cynthia, so your Mum's brothers are aware of the situation."

"And Drew?"

"Someone has also called upon Drew and Morag."

"Thankyou," said Alex graciously, "I wouldn't want to be the one to break the news."

They walked into the frozen night leaving the sanctuary of the vicarage behind them.

Those remaining in the house quickly knuckled down to assist with the chores. Ben and Rachel helped Miranda with the washing up and Justin ably supervised any necessary furniture moving operations, while Hilary and Annelie cleared away debris and tidied up so that all was spick and span for the Vicar's family in readiness for Christmas morning.

It had been arranged for Miranda to sleep-over in the guest room so that she was on hand to support Mrs Darnell in any way possible the following day leaving the Vicar free to concentrate on Church matters. At the moment Miranda had her own heartache to contend with so, being actively occupied, helping someone else was probably the best antidote for her. Her marriage was in a fragile state and she was finding it hard to come to terms with her husband, Matty's, infidelity and fraudulent practises. She was pleased to be busy. With so many willing hands the tasks were soon completed, goodbyes said, and the vicarage occupants settled down to sleep.

Hugh looked with sadness and compassion at the bruised face and stitched head of his sleeping wife as in prayer he opened his broken heart on behalf of his grieving parishioners and took comfort in the words of Isaiah, "O Lord be gracious to us, we long for you. Be our strength every morning, our salvation in time of distress," prayed by the prophet so long ago. Then, he settled to rest, in the knowledge that they were all held in the loving hands of an almighty God.

A few hours later the stillness of the night was broken by a child's voice, in a house across the Green, a stone's throw from the vicarage.

"Wow!" Seven year old Daniel Catton exclaimed bouncing on the end of his bed. He'd woken early full of excitement knowing that today was Christmas morning. In the dark he fumbled for the stocking he had hung, with Laura's help, the night before. It was heavy. His fingers explored the outside and he could feel interesting knobbly things inside. He dislodged it from the end of his bed and trundled it along the landing to the girls' room. They were both still asleep so he tiptoed out knowing if he woke them up he would be in trouble.

His exuberance often got him into trouble and Dad had warned him last night that he wasn't to wake Kirsty or Poppy this morning. Adam and Laura knew it was going to be an exciting day and wanted the children to have their proper sleep and wake up naturally so that they didn't become over tired or too fractious to enjoy the day. But Daniel desperately wanted to share his find with someone. Tentatively, he pushed open the door to Adam and Laura's room. They, too, were fast asleep following the late activities of the previous evening.

Disappointed, he bumped the stocking down the stairs, counting each one as he descended. He knew there were thirteen and he didn't want to miss a step. When he reached the bottom he made his way into the lounge. It was dark but even standing on tiptoe his fingers would not reach the light switch. For a moment he wondered what to do. Then he inched his way along the wall and behind the long curtains drawn across the French windows.

Daniel pressed his face to the glass and peered out into the darkness. He was surprised at the brightness reflecting back from the garden. Everywhere was white, covered with a blanket of snow. Snow! His eyes opened wider. Excitedly he thought *we can build a snowman*. He tried to open the door but, of course, it was locked. Daniel looked upon the tranquil scene with vexation and kicked the door frame viciously. However, the peaceful dawn of Christmas Day unfurled at its own pace with little concern for his youthful feelings. It had seen centuries of boyhood tantrums. One more made very little difference.

Frustrated, he turned back into the room. In doing so he left the curtains adrift thus creating a slim shaft of light which enabled him to identify objects in the room. His eyes, having grown accustomed to the diminished light, lit up in delight when he spied the Christmas tree. He remembered where the plug was pushed into the socket along the skirting board behind the tree. He flicked the switch. Instantly, the Christmas tree became a blaze of colour made up of myriad tiny bulbs of light, some static, others flashing intermittently. With wonder he watched the changing mosaic of colour. Still clutching his stocking he sank to the floor. In a short time the mesmeric influence of the lights caused his eyes to grow heavy and soon he was fast asleep.

That was where Laura found him a couple of hours later, sprawled at the foot of the tree amongst the Christmas presents. She smiled tenderly at the sight of her first born, a precious gift, in such a position. Silently she reached out to the mantelpiece to pick up the camera Adam had placed in readiness to capture special moments, such as this, of the children on this particular day. This was an instant worthy of embracing for posterity, at least in her mind.

Just along the lane, Roy Durrant stood by his sun-lounge window looking at, but not really seeing, the wintry scene across the garden rolling down to the marshes and the harbour beyond, cup in hand. Both he and Bernice had risen before the dawn of this Christmas morning. Neither had been able to sleep following Tom Catchpole's visit to tell them the news about the tragic accident to Val and Mick.

They spoke of days gone by when they were young. Roy remembered the joy of his parents when Valerie was born, a girl after two boys, six years his junior; a pretty, clever girl who never wanted to be left out of the boys' activities; tagged along whether it was football or cricket, swimming or gigs at the Corn exchange. She was never boyish, more like a mother hen, checking their kit was intact or they'd got enough food. No one was surprised when he met and fell in love with Bernice de Vessey. She was his soul mate but the astute could identify in her the same caring nature he had enjoyed in his relationship with his sister. Even after Roy and Bernice married Val continued to bake for them. He had sampled all her concoctions long before they became best sellers in Kemp's village store; "Unpaid taste tester, that's what I am," he teased.

He and Mick had rubbed along together throughout their school days. They were both products of enterprising and hardworking forebears, though each had gone through a phase of rebellion, he becoming an errand boy for the Village Stores during his teens and Mick commencing an apprenticeship with Durrant's, Master builders, after leaving school. However, family loyalty ensured they assumed their rightful mantle, when their respective fathers passed on to their heavenly reward, and each learned how to maintain a successful business in a fluctuating economic climate.

Roy could hear Bernice pottering in the kitchen and presumed she was making breakfast as well as tackling the preliminary preparations for Christmas dinner. He put his head around the door.

"Bernie, dear, I really don't think I could manage a big breakfast this morning. Do you mind? Would it be alright to have toast and marmalade?"

"Yes, of course, my dear. I've been stuffing the turkey so haven't started on breakfast yet. I think I'll join you in the same. I don't fancy a cooked breakfast, either."

She deftly manoeuvred the turkey into a baking tin, covered it in foil and placed it in the oven, washed her hands, made a fresh pot of tea and put a few slices of bread into the toaster. With an uncharacteristic sigh, Bernice sat down on a chair at the table opposite Roy. He looked at her with concern, stretched across the table and tenderly squeezed her hand. No words were necessary. Each was aware of the other's need and heart reached out to heart with compassion and understanding through that simple gesture, the culmination of shared seasoned maturity.

So, in silence they ate their breakfast absorbed in thoughts chiefly dominated by the appalling crash that had robbed them so cruelly of well-loved members of their family, and its ramifications for Alex and Emma and, on a wider scale, the village.

Daybreak, at the Castleton home on Christmas morning, was heralded by Bethany's early morning wake-up cry. As soon as he heard his daughter, Graeme slithered out of bed and adroitly tiptoed from the bedroom determined not to disturb Alex. He wanted her, and Emma, to sleep for as long as possible so that they were sufficiently rested in mind and body, equipped with inner resources, to cope with the grief they would experience when they awoke. Doctor Cooper had prescribed medication for both Alex and Emma the night before to enable them to sleep following the harrowing news of their parents' death. Despite her aching heart, after the initial shock, Alex became prayerfully composed but Emma grew increasingly embittered and distressed.

"Her anger is obliterating her grief," John Cooper had said by way of explanation.

However, by the time the girls and their companions had finally arrived home, following the candle-light service, Emma's behaviour was quite worrying and when Graeme first saw her he was most alarmed by the aggressive display of negative feelings. Doctor John pulled Graeme to one side, "You take care of Alex, my man, Trixie and I will deal with Emma. She is taking this very hard."

Emma overheard him and screamed hysterically, "Don't patronize me."

The Doctor slapped her cheek and pushed her firmly into a chair. Trixie slipped onto the arm of the chair and put her arms round Emma's taut shoulders. How her heart grieved for this lovely young woman. *Dear Father God, cradle her and comfort her in such a way that she may find rest in Your loving arms. Help us to love her through this loss,* she silently prayed. John drew up a stool and sat on it so that he was level with Emma.

He picked up the clenched fist from her lap, encased it gently in both of his own hands, and looked into her angry eyes. "Emma, you and I need to talk, but tonight it's more important that you sleep. It's going to be difficult so I'm going to give you something that will help. Will you take some tablets or shall I give you an injection?"

Her free hand reached up to the tingling cheek; her sullen glance at him a reminder that he had inflicted the pain. She nodded. John surprised by the sudden compliance, administered her sleeping pills. Afterwards, Trixie settled her down for the night.

"Sleep now, my dear, our prayers are with you." Trixie carefully pushed Emma's hair back from her face, leaned forward, and kissed her brow.

Thankfully, the rest of the night passed in undisturbed oblivion, his wife and sister-in-law not stirring.

Now, Graeme busied himself with Bethany's early morning routine; her young life oblivious to the sorrow that engulfed her family or the significance of the day. When she was fed, dressed and happily playing with her toys he snatched a few quiet moments, sat with a mug of tea watching his precious daughter, praying for wisdom to handle the fragile emotions of Alex and Emma when they eventually awoke.

CHAPTER EIGHT

The white Christmas that greeted the waking villagers was received with mixed reactions. Generally, the young were intent on enjoying the pleasures of the snow whilst the more circumspect and sedate were anxious for it to clear and be gone.

Similarly, mixed emotions welcomed Christmas morning. Some homes, such as the Cattons' and the Andamans', for different reasons, overflowed with happiness, whilst others, chiefly those related to the Kemps, were overwhelmed with sadness.

Somehow, the mysterious village grapevine, working with a life of its own, ensured that everyone was aware of all the tragic happenings of Christmas Eve so that very few remained untouched or unsympathetic toward those who were hurting. Typically, Ben Durrant had had the foresight to suggest a change of time for the morning service anticipating, that because of these events, many would oversleep and characteristically, this had been telegraphed throughout the community so that when Hugh entered the pulpit at a quarter past eleven he was staggered to see a packed church.

Christmas morning always attracted a good congregation but this morning surpassed all expectations. Peek, the verger, quite unfazed by the influx, brought in extra benches from the belfry dusting them down briskly with his cap, sending spiders scurrying to find protection elsewhere. He collected up some hassocks and suggested that the younger children sit on them in the aisles thus allowing room for more bodies to be squeezed into the pews. The children, unaware of health and safety issues, thought this great fun, the floor providing a larger play area for trying out their new toys.

For the second time in two days Hugh knew that the message, so thoughtfully prepared for the service, was inappropriate and in the vestry he prayed for words that would adequately meet the needs of the bleeding and suffering hearts of his congregation. He had insisted that Penny stay at home this morning but she had been equally adamant that she was attending the service despite her broken arm, stitches and bruises, "I want to give thanks. I may be sore but I am alive."

His heart was humbled too, when he saw Alex and Emma in the congregation seated alongside a subdued Roy and Bernice, but he was utterly astounded when his eye moved along the row and picked out Gordon and Cynthia Durrant and their wayward son, Matty. How long since they had been in Church? Matty's wedding to Miranda, I expect, but even then they hadn't been regular attendees, not even for high days and holidays. How sad that it took a tragedy to bring them through the doors of the Church. What would it take for them to embrace the teaching of the Church and become full members of the family of God? He prayed for them, and the girls, in his heart, as the choir concluded the Introit.

In the stillness of the Church, Graeme reflected on the early morning incidents at home, weighing up whether he had handled the situation sensitively or high-handedly. He honestly believed he had acted in the best interests of the family, in a manner that was honouring to God, influenced by the dictates of his heart. He had been very firm with Emma when, on waking, she maintained a sullen and argumentative attitude flatly refusing to go to Church.

"I am not going. Why should I?" she pouted petulantly.

"We are going, together, as a family," he stated quietly but firmly. "Many people are praying for us and supporting us. At this time we need one another and we need our friends. We are sticking together, Emma. It is in circumstances like these that our faith comes to the fore. We must practice what we believe. No matter what we are feeling at the moment, we must allow our faith to lift our feelings and trust in our Living God to see us through."

"Don't preach at me," she snapped angrily.

"I'm not, but this is the greatest challenge, to our faith, that any of us have experienced. We can't see our way through the dark tunnel, at the moment, but we've got to trust that God knows His way through or we're lost. How we behave today may also have a profound effect on someone who is seeking or even floundering in their faith."

"So, it's stiff upper lip and best foot forward from the Kemp clan?" Emma remarked sarcastically, tossing her auburn head back defiantly.

Graeme, careful not to show any emotion, rejoiced inwardly; here was a spark of the old Emma, definitely more preferable to the earlier tetchiness.

"No, not exactly, but displaying to the world a united front will show that although our hearts are broken we're trusting in a God who loves us and will meet our needs of this moment."

"It's hard," she commented lamely.

"Yes, I know, but it's not wrong to cry, to grieve or even be angry but it is wrong to deny God's power to help us come through this experience."

Emma glared at him, "Don't speak to me as though I'm a child in Sunday School," she snapped defensively at him.

"Then stop behaving like one."

As rage darkened her countenance Graeme regretted his retort so softly pleaded, "Please, Emma."

Angrily she tossed her head and stamped her foot, "Right, I'll get ready, as you command, then," she replied tartly and stomped her way huffily to her room.

In his pew Graeme nodded his head contemplatively as his heavy heart gave grateful thanks for the comforting presence of the Lord.

In contrast, across the aisle sat the Andaman family, the joy in their hearts reflected on their faces. Prayers had been answered, burdens lifted, Nicky found, alive if somewhat battered; they had much to give thanks to God for. Hugh expected to see Ben, his right hand man, with Rachel, his wife and their children but was pleasantly surprised to also see his in-laws, Doug and Christina Ransome amongst the congregation, as well as Lettie Milner, Doug's sister. *Wonders will never cease*, he thought, *no wonder Dave and Jansy look so happy*. Hugh was sure it wasn't just their engagement that caused such radiance; their anti-Christian relatives had come with them to Church. Cousin Annette's face, too, glowed with delight. *Thankyou, Father, for her sincere Christian witness. What a tremendous ambassador she is!*

Hugh was startled out of his prayerful reverie by the silence in the Church. He didn't know how long the choir had been in place. He gazed across the sea of expectant faces. He quaked in his shoes. How could he, a mere man, meet the diversity of their needs? His body trembled and he reached out to the lectern to support himself. He closed his eyes, opened his mouth, and poured out his heart to the Father God.

As one the congregation knelt silently in prayer. As the Vicar prayed many in the congregation identified with his words. Hugh was voicing their concerns, their petitions, and their thanksgivings. Hearts reiterated affirmations. There was an awesome sense of the presence of God. Hugh made God real; his prayer bringing God to them.

How can he know what I'm thinking? thought Miranda, shuffling uncomfortably in her seat.

That's what I'm feeling, right now, assented Emma, *very, very angry.*

I'm so confused by what's happening in the village, but the Vicar makes it sound as though God can make sense of it all, a baffled Melvin reflected.

Peace? Mmm, yes, there is peace. Thankyou, Father, whispered Bernice.

Even the curious and sceptical had cause to think the Vicar was speaking to someone who was present with him. Gordon Durrant shifted his position and looked to see where He was.

After a fervent "Amen", following Hugh's prayer, the Lord's Prayer was prayed with such reverence and feeling, not the meaningless, monotone repetition that was the wont of many, it brought tears to Alex's eyes. *Our Father, in heaven... Mum and Dad are with you, there...for ever, Amen.*

The congregation sat back in their seats, alert and expectant. Alex brushed away her tears. Seeing the action, Graeme took her hand and gently squeezed her fingers. She looked up at him and smiled her thanks for his understanding. He smiled back; a private moment of love and oneness between grieving husband and wife in the presence of their Father God.

But the brief tender glance did not go unnoticed. Jansy saw it, moved closer to Dave, and put her arm through his. Doctor John witnessed it and thanked God for His healing power. Miranda Durrant observed it with longing and regret at the broken relationship with Matty, *if only...* Miss Pedwardine tut tutted that such intimacy was not for public display. Annelie Durrant ogled with jealousy because no one looked at her like that. Annette Andaman thought how wonderful to be so loved by God and a man.

Hugh brought their erring thoughts back to the present by asking, "Why have you come this morning?"

"Certainly not for comfort," remarked Christina Ransome to Doug, restlessly moving her position on the hard pew.

"Shew yew my power ranger," shouted Darren Saunders excitedly from his temporary floor seat in the nave.

Irresponsible waste of money, thought Jennifer Pedwardine, remembering from her days as headmistress how difficult it had been to get the Saunders children's dinner money paid each week, but Penny Darnell smiled at her ten year old son, Gareth, knowing that the toy in question had been a much loved play fellow he had parted with reluctantly even though he was now too old for it, glad he was able to see the pleasure it was bringing to another little boy.

Hugh seized this unplanned response to invite all the children to the front of the Church. In turn they came up to him at the lectern and proudly displayed their Christmas gifts. Then he said to them, "I would like you all to sit at the foot of the altar and quietly play or hold your Christmas presents."

Hugh turned back to the congregation.

"Whatever your feelings, whatever your reasons for coming to Church this morning, this service is held to celebrate a gift, the greatest gift ever given to you and me; given because God loves you. So, will you join me in celebration? Let us unwrap this gift together."

Hugh could hear the strains of the organ playing softly in the background; he paused and picked out the melody of "Away in a manger." He was glad Stuart Jenner was organist today. Stuart was always attune to the mood of a service. His sensitivity enabled him to adapt and make adjustments to the agreed plan for the service. Thankfully, temperamental, Mrs Esmeralda Dandridge, the regular organist, had been invited to spend Christmas with her daughter in Yorkshire. Had she been organist today she would have been belting out the "Calypso Carol" by now and the thought provoking atmosphere would have been lost. Time enough for rousing melodies. The gentle lullaby, chosen by Stuart, enabled Hugh to encourage the congregation to focus on the baby Jesus.

"The children are enjoying the gifts, you have chosen and given them, in a variety of ways. How will you enjoy the gift God gives to you today? Like Mary, ponder it in your heart, as you sing these familiar words."

*   *

"Emma, dear, would you set out some mince pies and open up this tin of shortbread, for me, please? Plates are in the top cupboard on the right. I don't know about you but I'm beginning to feel rather peckish. Although we were up early we only had a light breakfast and it will be a little while before dinner is ready."

The kitchen door opened. Bernice looked round. "Oh, Justin, you're just the man for this job. Could you carry the tray through to the sitting room for me? I'll bring the cream and sugar and Emma will manage the plates and mince pies." Ever the gentleman Justin complied with his mother's request.

In the sitting room Roy and Graeme were discussing the numbers in Church for the service. Alex was crouched down on the carpet playing with Bethany.

"Ben said it was an unprecedented number for Christmas morning, not just the regulars but spasmodic attendees, as well as a fair few who don't normally darken the doors of the Church," commented Roy.

"Come to gloat," spluttered Emma bitterly.

"I'm sure that's not true, dear," said Bernice gently.

"I agree," responded Alex, "I believe the village came to offer our family its support. I for one was really encouraged by the way folk rallied round us."

"Yes," said Graeme, "the most unexpected people came up to us at the conclusion of the service to voice their concern and proffer their comfort and promise of prayer. Lord Edmund waited in the wings while Mr Baxter, in his normal unwholesome state, held Alex's hand and stuttered his condolences. Then, when the coast was clear, Lord Edmund put his arms round both Alex and Emma and expressed his deep regret."

"Bless his heart, he, of all people, can genuinely empathise with our feelings," murmured Bernice remembering the tragic motor-bike accident, fifteen years earlier, that had robbed her brother of his son and the subsequent untimely death of his heart-broken wife.

"Miss Pedwardine was almost human as she expressed her sympathy."

"Dad said we'd see her begin to mellow now she's retired perhaps this is the start."

"Mrs Jenner, for once, was lost for words. She just held my arm briefly and muttered, "Sorry" but there were tears streaming down her face."

"Those two women from the Common, who were in the shop warring together yesterday afternoon, came up to me," said Emma, "Good sort yew're Dad an' yew're Mum a pretty fair cook," said one. "Stores won't be the same wi'out 'em. Village won't be the same wi'out the Stores," said the other. It was quite a contradiction of their vociferous opinions of yesterday."

"Tragedy brings people up with a start. Makes them look at things in a different light," said Roy quietly.

"Little Kirsty Catton offered me one of her Christmas sweets so that I wouldn't be sad because my Mummy's gone to Heaven then her brother, Daniel, came barging in and said it would be alright when I died because then we'd see each other again," said Alex.

"Children can be so brutally forthright, can't they?" declared Bernice.

"Yes, Aunt Bernice, they're always open and honest, no covering up and I'm afraid this little lady is no exception." Alex picked up her whimpering daughter. "She's telling us she's hungry. Would you mind if I fed her now then she'll settle down for her sleep and we'll be able to enjoy our meal without interruption?"

"Of course, my dear, just make yourself at home. I expect she's unsettled, too, because this isn't home, not her home, I mean. Is there anything you need?" Bernice hovered like a mother hen around Alex and Bethany but Graeme had already anticipated his daughter's needs and was in the kitchen making the necessary preparations for her lunch.

Whilst the little girl was being fed Bernice attended to the finishing touches to the Christmas meal. Roy sat in quiet contemplation by the log fire in the sitting room. Emma wandered into the sun-lounge. After he had carried the trays of crockery into the kitchen for his mother Justin joined her.

Both of them stood for a while silently looking out of the window at the wintry scene.

The weather and the accident had completely altered the carefully arranged plans that had been made for sharing Christmas with family. When Sergeant Tom Catchpole had first broken the news to Graeme he had rung his own parents in Norwich to acquaint them with the situation. They in turn decided not to travel the thirty odd miles to Newton Westerby in view of the icy conditions so were spending Christmas Day with Graeme's sister and family who lived only a few streets away from them. On Boxing Day morning they would make a reassessment of travelling conditions. If the snow cleared they would come over early in the day. But Bernice didn't like the idea of Alex and Graeme, and Emma, spending Christmas Day without the support of family so in her loving way she had persuaded them that their presence in her home would be a great comfort to her and Uncle Roy.

Justin was the first to break the silence.

"How are you, Em?" he gently asked his cousin.

"What do you think?" Emma snapped back at him, without turning round, her entire body tensing stiffly. "My parents have just died and you ask how I am! How do expect me to be? Over the moon?" she spat out sarcastically. "If you really want to know, I'd like to kick the living daylights out of whoever killed them."

"Em, you've really got to stop blaming everyone else for the accident and..."

"Now you sound like Graeme," Emma rudely interrupted but Justin continued as though she hadn't butted in, "...your behaviour last night, particularly towards Doctor Cooper, was completely out of order."

"Don't you dare tell me how to behave," she hissed through clenched teeth. She tossed her auburn head and turned to face him, hands on hips, feet planted defiantly, her lips pursed and her eyes blazing."Nor tell me to forgive their killers!"

Justin held her gaze unwaveringly. Then, choosing his words with great care said "Em, whichever way you look at it you can't get away from the fact that you acted appallingly then and you are continuing to do so now."

"How dare you speak to me like that?"

"I dare because I care for you, Em."

She shrugged her shoulders. "You've no idea, absolutely no idea at all, how I feel or what I'm going through." She hung her head forlornly, the black mood, that had descended upon her when the news of her parents death had broken, very much in evidence.

"Don't be so pathetic, Em, it's unbecoming and not worthy of you."

Her chin rose in the air, defiantly. "What do you mean?"

"Your parent's accident is a dreadful shock to us all and I can understand how devastated you feel but taking your anger out on friends and family, who despite their own distraught feelings are offering their loving support, is totally unacceptable."

Emma stamped her foot as a further spark of anger ignited within her.

"I'm not answerable to anyone, least of all you, about my actions or my conversation," she yelled contemptuously.

"So you deny the words of Psalm 19, Emma?"

Justin paused to let his words sink in then quietly reiterated the psalmist's prayer, *"May the words of my mouth and the meditation of my heart be acceptable in your sight, O Lord."*

She looked at him coldly.

Justin's heart turned over within him at the bleakness displayed on her face. *O Lord, may she feel Your love and compassion reaching out to her,* he prayed silently.

"Why does everyone keep quoting the Bible to me?" Emma asked in exasperation.

"It's the Word of God. It confirms His promise to be with us at all times."

"Empty words, worthless promises," she muttered despondently, with a scowl on her face.

"Oh, my dear Emma, to the children of God they are the most precious assurances we have. I know that Aunt Val and Uncle Mick believed them with all their hearts and today, although their bodies are broken, their spirits live on in eternity with the Lord they love. For us, left behind, the parting is hard and the manner in which you have been separated from your Mum and Dad is not one you would have chosen but we believe God's timing is right."

"I can't accept that," Emma snapped back at him.

"Ecclesiastes tells us there is a time for everything, a time to be born and even a time to die. God has a unique lifespan for each of us and, when we live in the will of God we know that at a time that is right for Him, He will call us home to be with him forever. The earthly work of Aunt Val and Uncle Mick is complete. Someone else will need to continue what they have started…"

"But I don't want to work in the Stores", Emma pouted, "I've got other plans."

"I was thinking more of the spiritual influence".

"Oh," she shrugged, "you mean in the house groups and fellowships at Church?"

"Yes. Aunt Val and Aunt Mick not only lived out their Christian faith in their work-a-day life by showing compassion as well as integrity in their dealings with people in the Village Stores but they fulfilled a particular ministry in the Church. Your Mum was gifted in hospitality and many feel welcome in the Church family and your Dad was active in the men's group and the tape fellowship.

"I can't do that." Emma quipped emphatically.

"You're not expected to. We don't appoint ourselves to do God's work. Those whom He calls know how they should respond. I'm sure the Lord has it all in hand so we'll leave it with Him to sort out. For the moment I'm more concerned about you," Justin reached out and placed his hand upon her arm.

"Oh?" Emma looked up at him defiantly.

"Emma, what are you afraid of? You appear to have no peace about your parent's eternity. It seems to me that you've let fear and anger usurp your trust and faith in God." Justin paused to let his words sink in. As he watched her face Emma's expression changed and Justin felt her begin to relax. He moved his arm around her shoulders and drew her close to him. Gently he said "I know you so well, Em. Over the years, as family, we've spent a lot of time together. You've always been the younger sister I longed for but never had.

"Throughout that time I observed your constant struggle with pride and persistent unwillingness to acknowledge that you were a sinner in need of salvation but it was here, not so very long ago, sitting with Mum, that you repented of your sin and accepted Jesus Christ as your Saviour and I witnessed your conversion. The certainty in your heart glowed on your face and the change in your behaviour was remarkable. It was lovely to see. You were so eager to grow as a Christian; you always had your Bible in your hand and were forever asking questions.

"Our wonderful God of love worked that miracle in your life and He's still the same. He hasn't changed."

As he spoke, Justin could feel Emma's body throbbing and hear her throat catching. Quietly he continued, "When we are faced with tragedy Em, He doesn't desert us. Time and time again in His word He promises to comfort us and to be with us. Do you remember when we were studying the Gospel of Matthew in house group; we learned that Jesus himself said "Blessed are those who mourn for they will be comforted." Also, David the Psalmist wrote, "Even though I walk through the valley of the shadow of death...You are with me," because he'd proved this to be true. "I am with you always," Jesus promises us, in faith we believe and accept the assurance of His words."

Emma turned in his arms and sobbed uncontrollably on his shoulder. With tender-hearted understanding, Justin held her as the pent up emotion of grief was released. Silently he prayed for her. After a few moments he raised his eyes and saw the bowed heads of his family. He was heartened by the sight. *Thankyou, Father God, for my believing family and the tower of strength they are.*

Unbeknown to either Justin or Emma, the family had joined Roy, around the fire in the sitting room, and were quietly upholding the young couple in prayer. Whilst Alex had fed and settled Bethany for her nap, Graeme had carved the turkey as Bernice served up the vegetables into tureens. When they realised the heart-searching conversation going on in the sun-lounge, although the meal was ready to serve, they turned the oven down low and put everything in to keep warm and gave their prayerful support to the battle waging in Emma's heart.

At that juncture Roy lifted his head and caught his son's eye. With keen sensitivity Roy stood, tapped Graeme, Bernice and Alex on the shoulder and indicated that they should join Justin and Emma in the sun-lounge.

Placing his hand upon Emma, Roy opened his heart in prayer. "Our Gracious, Heavenly Father, You see our broken hearts and in our pain and loss, we claim Your promise to heal the heartbroken. Pour into our lives Your comfort and peace. You are our hiding place, our refuge, and our ever present help in time of trouble. May we know we are held securely in Your everlasting arms of love; that You are in control at this time. We honour You and accept Your grace through Jesus Christ, our Living Lord, Amen."

After a little while Emma lifted her head, stepped away from Justin and found five pairs of eyes upon her. A heartrending gasp escaped through her mouth. Tears again filled her eyes and threatened to gush like a waterfall down her face. Her shoulders heaved. She sighed. As she brushed aside the persistent tears she scanned each precious face, a sense of peace flooded her heart and a tentative smile reached her lips.

"Oh Em." Alex threw her arms around her sister who clung to her with such intensity she thought her neck would break.

"Alex, I've been so faithless and doubting. It's been so hard. Please forgive me for being so horrid and churlish."

Alex started to interrupt but Emma put up her hand. "No, let me finish. I'm really sorry for causing so much extra pain and hurt, Alex. Whatever would Dad say? He'd be so ashamed of me, wouldn't he? I feel I've let him and Mum down very badly." She hung her head and shook it slowly.

Knowing how much such an expression of regret cost Emma, Alex responded graciously, "Em, Dad would understand and he would be proud of you now. To acknowledge you were wrong and ask forgiveness is the new Emma, not the old unregenerate one."

Emma's sniffs increased accompanied by rasping sobs and she fumbled around for a hankie.

"Here you are, dear," Bernice, ever the consummate housewife, handed her a box of tissues.

Alex waited while Emma regained her composure then quietly added, "For a time, grief obscured God's redeeming grace in your life but I trust you now realise what a wonderful God we have, who is the rich source of every mercy, comfort and strength."

Some time later, after more tears, embraces and prayer, Bernice, in her tender-hearted manner gathered her grieving family together. She was anxious to share with them, the Christmas meal she had so lovingly prepared, before it became spoiled beyond all recognition.

CHAPTER NINE

"Your turn, Dad," shouted Gareth excitedly. Miranda could hear considerable hilarity coming from the vicarage sitting room, where the Vicar's family were enjoying a game of Uno, a Christmas stocking gift Gareth had opened earlier in the day. She was in the kitchen attending to the Christmas meal. Fortunately, Penny Darnell had got well ahead with preparations on Christmas Eve, prior to her accident, so all Miranda had to do was turn on the oven to cook the chicken and vegetables. Dessert was a choice of Valerie Kemp's delicious Christmas puddings, traditional, the Vicar's preference or the ice-cream version, the children's favourite. Miranda insisted Mrs Darnell rest, with a cup of coffee, on her return from the morning service, adamant she could cope with the meal. Ellie was in a helpful mood and cheerfully set the table and organized the Vicar in the placement of chairs before they were roped in to play the game with Gareth.

Carefully, Miranda basted the chicken, turned the roast potatoes and checked the vegetables. She was just placing a baking tray, containing the devils-on-horseback and chestnut stuffing balls, on the top shelf in the oven when urgent hammering on the back door made her jump. Quickly finishing her task she answered the door to find Mr Peek standing there, breathless and agitated, cap in hand.

"Hello, Mr Peek, can I help you?" Miranda asked with a smile.

"Is Vicar there? Mus' come. Quick."

Miranda nodded; being the Doctor's receptionist she was used to dealing with people who wanted things done quickly, if not sooner.

"Step inside Mr Peek. I'll let the Vicar know you're here," she said kindly and walked calmly through to the sitting room to inform the Vicar of his visitor. Hugh followed Miranda back to the kitchen and greeted his verger.

After a brief, frenetic conversation Hugh made to accompany Peek across to the Church. As he stepped out of the door he turned back to Miranda and said, "I won't be long. I hope dinner won't spoil for another ten minutes."

Miranda smiled and said, "Not at all, Vicar."

"Good," and was gone.

Hearing the kitchen door close, Penny Darnell gingerly eased her bruised body from the chair in the sitting room, and cautiously made her way to the kitchen to investigate.

"How is it going, Miranda?" she enquired.

"Fine, Mrs Darnell. We'll be ready to serve in about fifteen minutes or when the Vicar gets back from the Church."

"That will be lovely and very well timed. I really appreciate your cheerful readiness to help us out."

"You're more than welcome. I'm really enjoying it. I wouldn't get a chance to cook at home with Mum and Hilary vying to outdo one another."

Penny looked puzzled. "But I thought Hilary was vegetarian," she commented.

"Oh, she is, but it's important to her to prove that not only are veggie dishes healthier but also they are tastier than meat dishes. So, she's trying to outdo Mum with her veggie version of Christmas dinner. Not surprisingly Dad won't budge. How can he, being a butcher? Mum enjoys both but really prefers meat. Jacky will eat anything as long as it's food. I'm afraid I'm probably on Dad's side. I do enjoy my roast dinners," Miranda grinned.

Penny nodded and said with a smile, "It's a good thing we're all different."

"Yes, it does make life interesting."

"Muu...mm!" Their conversation was cut short as Gareth shouted and burst energetically through the kitchen door. "When's dinner? I'm starving!"

Penny raised her eyebrows, "Are you really?"

"We...ell! Perhaps not starving," he agreed sheepishly knowing how strict his mother was on truthfulness, "but my tummy's growling and I do feel hungry."

Penny put her uninjured arm around his shoulders. "It won't be long now. As soon as Dad gets back we'll sit down. Would you like to get the matches and light the candles on the dining table for me?"

His eyes lit up. "Ooh, yes Mum," thrilled at being trusted with such responsibility. He found the long handled safety matches on the shelf and accompanied his mother to the dining room eager to demonstrate his expertise.

As Miranda strained the vegetables and tipped them into serving bowls Ellie wandered into the kitchen. Miranda looked up, "Hi, there," then, concentrating on the job in hand she placed the chicken onto the large oval meat platter.

"Can I help?" asked Ellie tentatively.

"Would you like to arrange the roast potatoes, stuffing balls and devils-on-horseback around the chicken?" Miranda then returned the vegetable dishes to the warm oven and started to mix the gravy.

"Why are they called devils-on-horseback?" Ellie asked as she commenced her task. Miranda laughed.

"I have absolutely no idea. I'll have to ask my Mum, she'll probably know."

"It's a daft name for mini sausages wrapped in bacon held together with a prune laden cocktail stick," Ellie exclaimed.

"Yes it is, but they are very tasty."

"Mmm, I like them," she agreed. "But I don't like the devils who attacked my Mum," Ellie muttered under her breath.

"Ellie!" Miranda gasped, shocked at her words, spoken so bitterly.

"The Devil's wicked and Mum's attackers were wicked in what they did to her," she explained.

Before Miranda could reply, the front door banged and shortly afterwards Hugh came bounding into the kitchen to announce his return.

"Can we manage another plate, Miranda?"

"Yes Vicar, no problem"

"Good."

He stood squarely in front of his daughter and placed a hand upon her shoulder.

"Ellie, we have a guest for dinner. Could we set another place?"

"Sure, Dad. I think I've finished here."

She looked questioningly at Miranda, who nodded, so Ellie made her way through to the dining room.

"We're ready to eat whenever you are, Miranda," Hugh said before following to assist his daughter.

"Ellie," Hugh said quietly as they worked together to rearrange the seating and table settings, "our guest is another victim of the violence of the last few days. She has suffered much trauma and is very distressed. She is not her usual self but I know that you will treat her with kindness."

"Who is it Dad?" she asked hesitantly.

"Mrs Jenner", he replied.

"Oh, no," Ellie gulped in dismay.

"Ell...ie!" Hugh gently admonished; his eyes full of concern as they focused on his busy daughter.

Ellie completed her chore, surveyed her handiwork then, standing tall to her full 5' 1" height, she looked up to her father.

"It's OK, Dad. Mum lectured me yesterday on my behaviour towards those less fortunate than myself. I promise that I won't let you down. I'll behave impeccably and treat Mrs Jenner courteously."

"Thankyou, my dear," Hugh beamed at Ellie, then swiftly reduced the distance between them and hugged her affectionately. As he kissed the top of her head he gazed across the dining table.

"This all looks delightful. You have a real flare for artistic design," he complimented her with a twinkle in his eye, "it seems a shame to spoil it with messy dinner plates."

"Oh, Dad," she scolded light heartedly, as he teased her, but secretly she was pleased that he had taken notice of her efforts. Perhaps his opinion towards her choice of career was softening. *Maybe, by the time I sit for my GSCE exams, his point of view will be more favourable.* She sighed, content for the moment to bask in his praise.

In the sitting room Gareth reluctantly gathered together the playing cards from the unfinished game of Uno. He caught snatches of Penny's conversation with a subdued Mrs Jenner as she tried to make the older lady feel welcome and at ease. Mum was always kind and caring especially when people had problems, he thought. Even he could see that Mrs Jenner was not her normal chatty self. He'd tried to tell Mum yesterday, after the Christingle service, that he thought something was wrong. Now, the old lady could hardly utter a word, seemed very dejected and was constantly shivering, even though she still had on her coat, which oddly looked much too big for her.

Hugh had given only the briefest of explanations when he'd accompanied Mrs Jenner into the sitting room and introduced her as their dinner guest so Penny was completely in the dark concerning the circumstances, which had led to Mrs Jenner requiring sanctuary in their home. *Dear Lord, be all that Mrs Jenner needs at the moment. May she know Your loving arms around her and find in You the source of every comfort and blessing,* she quietly prayed, as she observed the distressed, dishevelled woman beside her. Penny put her hand upon her arm.

"My dear, Mrs Jenner, I'm so pleased you have come to our home to share the Christmas meal with our family."

Tears flooded the old lady's eyes.

"Oh, Mrs Darnell, bless yow'n heart for yow'n kindness but I've been so wicked that yew won't want to know me let aloan allow me near yow'n dear children." Unable to control the weeping, the floodgates opened, but before she could recover herself sufficiently to impart more of her story, Miranda rang a bell summoning everyone to "come and dine."

It was therefore many hours later before Penny learned the full account of Mrs Jenner's frightening experiences.

Peek had seen Mrs Jenner crying and distressed in the Church as he was putting things to rights following the Christmas morning service. Receiving no intelligible response to his blunt enquiries, he strode to the vicarage for reinforcements. When he returned with the Vicar they found Mrs Jenner huddled in the far corner by a radiator.

"She's bin 'ere a lot these last few days," Peek whispered in the Vicar's ear. Hugh gently probed and learned, between the sobs, that she had no food and had been without money with which to buy any for three weeks, her pension card having been taken. Yesterday, she was so desperate; she had been driven to take things from the shelves in the Village Stores and was now ridden with guilt. She was obviously very weak, hungry and cold. A quick assessment of her physical state and reading possible evil intent against her, between her faltering words, caused Hugh to make the decision to invite her to the vicarage for the Christmas meal, ring Doctor Cooper from the vestry and scribble a note to Sgt Tom Catchpole, instructing Peek to get it to him ASAP.

"I'll go afore I 'ave m'dinner. I dew believe 'e be at the Docs."

"Oh?"

"Yup, 'e should a' gone to 'is Mother's but the weather put paid to that. Mrs Cooper doan't like the idea of 'im spending Christmas Day on 'is own in that draughty ole police flat so invited 'im to dinner."

"That's good."

"Yup, good sort is Tom. 'e also changed shifts with that Inspector chap so's 'e could a spend Christmas wi' 'is family."

"I'd heard they'd set up the Doctor's waiting room as an incident room."

"Yup, 'e an' young Prettyman are taking statements from everyone as quick as ye like."

"I expect they want to sort out this sorry mess and bring the culprits to justice as soon as possible, for everyone's sake."

"Yup, it's a right rum dew!" The verger stroked his stubbly chin, thoughtfully. Then he put on his cap, turned and quickly made his way from the Church. "I'll be off then, Vicar," he called.

Hugh caught up with the retreating figure, placed his hand upon his shoulder and said with feeling, "Thankyou, my man; God bless you."

P.C. Prettyman's fingers flew across the keyboard as he typed up the statements they had taken earlier in the day. Tom Catchpole sat at the other end of the long table Dr Cooper had helped them set up in the waiting room which he had agreed could temporarily be turned into an incident room. He leaned back and, with his hands behind his head, ruminated over the rich amount of information they had already been given.

The Vicar had graciously allowed an announcement to be made following the Christmas morning service, asking for anyone with information to call into the Doctor's waiting room. No sooner had the service concluded than a steady stream of villagers came to them with their little bits of trivia and gossip. He and Prettyman speedily sifted out unrelated incidents from that which was clearly relevant to the matter in hand.

What initially proved puzzling was the number of crimes that appeared to have been committed during the last twenty-four hours. They seemed to have no bearing to one another, yet as the policemen painstakingly pieced the puzzle together, it was emerging that they could have been instigated by the same perpetrator, all different, all separate, yet, at the same time part of a whole. A clear picture was beginning to unfold.

"I've made a list of the reported crimes, sir."

"Right, now make columns and put in the names of those seen in the vicinity of each crime."

"Yes, sir." The young constable juggled his papers and carefully searched for the information his sergeant required. He filled in the columns and gradually the graph revealed constancy.

Tom slowly shook his head and said in soft tones to himself, "He's always there. He figures somewhere in them all. Is it him? Or has he been set up?"

Prettyman looked up at his colleague, "Sorry, sir?"

Deliberately Tom pointed to the pattern that Prettyman's graph exposed.

"We'll have to see the Kemp girls. I need a clearer sequence of events. Hopefully, they'll be able to help us there and also corroborate some of the times that certain people were in the Village Stores. I also want to talk to Michelle Cook, on her own. Joe butted in every time she attempted to answer my questions this morning."

He pushed his chair back and stood up. Observing his action, Prettyman nodded towards the clock on the waiting room wall. "Mrs Cooper is expecting us to go through for the Christmas meal in about ten minutes and most of the people we need to see will also be just sitting down to eat. Maybe we could go in about an hour or so?" the young constable suggested tentatively.

"You're right. No one's going anywhere. I've given Michelle Cook a mobile phone and my number to ring if Joe or Josh shows signs of leaving the house."

"I'm surprised that the Gov. released them. They're obviously guilty."

Tom raised his eyebrows and looked directly at the constable.

"Are they? Look who else be at the scene. Don't presume. We've got to prove it, bor. Circumstantial evidence won't convict them and, unless our case be rock solid, the Crown Prosecution Service will throw it out. We've got some hard graft ahead of us. Facts, facts, facts; corroborated facts. We've a lot of foot slogging and methodical paperwork to attend to, plus a pinch of Poirot's miraculous grey cells working on our behalf, before we can present our case with confidence."

"Stop it!" shouted Michelle Cook as she banged the dinner plates in front of her squabbling family. There was stunned silence, for despite tremendous provocation, Michelle was not known to raise her voice in anger. Maxine and the younger children shrank back in their seats alarmed but Josh picked up his cutlery and attacked his dinner ferociously. Joe nonchalantly shrugged his shoulders, and sniggered at her contemptuously, sensing he was the real cause for the outburst.

"Aw, come on, love," he cajoled "where's yow'n Christmas spirit?"

"I can't take noo more, Joe. I've had it up to here with yow'n thieving ways," Michelle indicated the top of her head as she spoke, "and what's more I'm putting my foot down. This be the last meal yew and our bor Josh get in this house till yew mend yow'n ways."

"Doan't talk such squit, girl."

"I'm not. It's the truth, Joe. This be the most sumptuous meal we've had in a long while and yew almost killed the hand that provided it."

"Yew doan't knoo what yew be on about."

"Yow'n thieving be bad enough but attacking people we knoo, good people who've never done us harm, I can't take that."

"Yew approves of snooping, in'erfering busybodies, then?"

"I disapprove of yew beating up innocent people."

"Even though they be a listenin' to our conversation?"

"She was just passing the doorway on her way home having delivered the turkey yew're now eating."

"Nosey-parker, more like."

"What on earth was yew discussing that called for such violence, National secrets?"

"Never yew mind."

"Well, I dew mind. Yow'n actions affect the whole of this family and I'm not putting up with that sort of behaviour any more. It be a bad influence on the children, teaching 'em wrongs things."

"Who says?"

"I dew."

"Oh, yew dew, dew yew? We'll see about that," Joe clattered his knife and fork on the plate, pushed back his chair and made to stand up, raising his clenched right hand in the air as he did so.

Michelle sat hunched up in her chair, and with the mobile phone Tom Catchpole had given her hidden in her lap, quickly tapped in the numbers she had memorised to contact him.

Joe didn't see the deft movement but thought she was cowering in the usual position she took before he hit her and strode towards her. She looked up and in a determined voice, that belied the fearful quivering she was experiencing, Michelle said, "Sit yew down, Joe."

Unused to retaliation, Joe stopped in his tracks, still intent on his action.

"Sit down, Joe," Michelle repeated firmly.

"Who dew yew think yew be telling what tew dew? Yew're m'wife and yew'll dew as I say not give me orders."

"Sit down, Joe," she said emphatically, her confidence increasing with each passing moment. "Yew will not hit me or our children ever again. The way yew has behaved over the last few days yew'll be lucky if yew see the children or me ever again."

"Aw, Michelle, stop this squit," he stepped menacingly towards her.

"Noo. I mean it, Joe. Sit down."

Somewhat stunned by her calm defiance and the force of her words Joe stood and gaped at Michelle. He'd never seen her like this and he wondered who'd put her up to it. His silence gave Michelle the opportunity to voice thoughts that had been building up within her for a long time.

"Yew're not the man I married, Joe. I don't knoo where the kind, caring Joe Cook from my wedding day is. He's lost, buried, disappeared, I don't knoo how else to describe it, but he's smothered by the thieving brute standing in front of me today, along with my love, patience, tolerance and every ounce of energy that I had. Because of yew families in our village are hurting and grieving this Christmas."

"Hey, hey, steady girl. What yew insinuatin'? I in't killed noo one."

"Haven't yew? Are yew sure, Joe?"

"'Course I'm sure."

"Vicar's wife asked for it," mumbled Josh, "and Nicky got what he deserved for non-cooperation."

"Nicky? Did yew say Nicky?"

"Aw, give it a rest, Mum; they all got what was due to 'em."

"I can't."

"Stingy, the lot of 'em."

"What on earth dew yew mean, Josh?"

"Shu'rup, Michelle. The bor's right, drop it. Those Kemps only got their just desserts."

Josh guffawed, "Good joke, that, Dad."

"I won't be quiet, Joe, for once yew just listen to me. In the service this morning the Vicar spoke about forgivin' those who've hurt us. Do yew know he forgives yew, Joe? I don't know how he can after what yew did to Mrs Darnell. I can't, Joe."

"Yew gone all religious, then?" sneered Joe. Michelle ignored the interruption and continued, "Neither yew nor Josh seem to have any regrets for the bad things yew've done, that makes it even harder for me to forgive yew. Now, sit yew down and finish yow'n dinner."

Still shocked by her stance Joe compliantly did as she bid. But, her orders had not ceased. For once, she had his attention, so she pressed home her point. "After yew've finished dinner yew and Josh will collect together all yow'n ill-gotten gains. If yow'n memory fails yew, I've made a list of all the things that doan't belong in this house. Then, yew, along with the evidence of yow'n crimes will leave this house for good."

"But Michelle..."

"Mumm..." Joe and Josh shouted in unison.

"Yew be as bad as 'is nibs and the starchy school marm. We sure took 'em down a peg or two." Josh guffawed again. Michelle stood her ground.

"Yew will. I told yew, I've had enough, and until yew be willing to rethink the way yew're living yew won't come back here. That's my final word on the matter."

Michelle prepared to eat her now cooling meal.

"Thomas, stop snivelling and eat up yow'n dinner."

"Bradley, sit on yow'n chair and wait for the rest of us to finish."

"Maxine, goo and get some kitchen roll and bloo yow'n nose, then give the custard a stir as yew pass the stove."

Giving orders to the children was familiar territory so Michelle relaxed to enjoy her food. However, Joe was at sixes and sevens, unsure how to handle a dominant wife. He sat down to finish his meal thinking over the threats she had made.

Meanwhile, outside the Cook house, Sgt Catchpole, with P.C. Prettyman hovered, listening in to the interaction between the different members of the Cook family. Tom was thankful that Michelle had remembered all his earlier instructions and activated the speaker button on the mobile phone. He had followed their conversation from the moment he received the call, just as he was finishing his Christmas lunch at the Cooper's, and prepared to take action should matters get out of hand. He didn't want to move in too soon but neither did he want Michelle or the children to be at risk if he acted too late. Carefully, he listened, trying to gage Joe Cook's mood. Tom's earlier deductions that the Cooks were implicated in the crimes in the village and possibly further afield were confirmed by the words from their own lips.

He called Inspector Capps at home.

"Sir, we're going to have to move today with regard to the Cook duo. Mrs Cook has issued an ultimatum and we have incriminating evidence on tape."

"Right, Sergeant. I've just received another communiqué from Northumbria police who are keenly interested in the pair. Bring them in."

Chapter Ten

Emma woke on Boxing Day morning refreshed in body, but all too soon a sinking feeling hit the pit of her stomach, and her emotions reeled as she recalled the devastating tragedy to her parents. Slowly she sat up in bed remembering the heart searching conversation with her cousin, Justin, and the time of sharing that followed with her Aunt and Uncle, Alex and Graeme as they wept and reminisced together.

Father God, You are so patient with Your children, she thought. *Although I've stopped blaming You for the crash I'm still struggling with this situation but You already know that. Please get me through today.* Reluctantly she recognised that He had stilled the anger that threatened to consume her and given her peace and assurance. *In Your time, indeed!* she mused. *Your time is always the right time although it doesn't always seem so to us. We question Your timing. I know I do.* Slowly Emma shook her head and softly asked, *Why couldn't You stop the accident happening? If You are the all-seeing, all-powerful God why couldn't You save them?*

She picked up her Bible, from the bedside cabinet, and flicked through the Old Testament pages looking for the chapter in Ecclesiastes Justin had referred to the previous afternoon, her mind still mulling over this thought. *God's timing is always right; right for whom? Me? Mum and Dad? I don't want to lose them.* Tears coursed uncontrollably down her cheeks. She grabbed at the bed sheet to scrub them away. *Did they want to die just then? I'm sure not, though I believe they were ready to meet the Lord, despite the fact that they enjoyed living for Him.* She pondered for a moment. *I think the apostle Paul wrote something about living being Christ but dying being the greater reward. I find that difficult to understand. I suppose it means eternity is the ultimate goal to be attained. I'll have to ask Graeme or Justin about it. Oh, Dad, why did you have to go now, when I need you so much. I've such a lot of questions that need answers.* The tears kept flowing like the relentless waves on the seashore. Emma sniffed as she brushed them away with the back of her hand but not before one or two had splashed onto the pages of her Bible.

"*Come on, Girl, pull yourself together,*" admonished a voice from the past.

"Yes, Dad," Emma responded sheepishly.

She took a deep breath to compose herself, drew a paper tissue from a box on the bedside cabinet to blow her nose, and started searching again. After a while she eventually found the verses in Ecclesiastes and quietly read them...*There is a time... I questioned your timing, Lord. I even denied its possibility. Father, forgive me for doubting your sovereign will over our lives, and my anger...* She couldn't continue along those thoughts because she suddenly remembered her conduct on Christmas Eve. Her feelings plummeted and her neck and cheeks flamed as she recalled her disgraceful behaviour towards Doctor John and the Vicar. Involuntarily, she covered the lower part of her face with her hands in embarrassment. "Oh, I'll have to go and apologise," she gasped. Emma jumped out of bed and hastily prepared to meet the day.

Completing her ablutions in record time Emma tore downstairs, grabbed her coat from the peg in the hallway and made her way to unlock the front door.

"You're in a hurry," a voice called from the kitchen, "have you had breakfast?"

Emma paused, then turned back, and rushed into the kitchen where her brother-in-law was sitting at the table.

"Oh, Graeme, I've just remembered how ill-mannered I was to the Vicar and Doctor John on Christmas Eve, so I'm just off to make amends," she said breathlessly.

Graeme glanced at the clock, then back to Emma and said, "Don't you think your apologies will be more acceptable if you waited a little longer when people might be up and about?"

Emma looked up at the clock on the kitchen wall.

"Oh! I didn't realise it was so early. I seem to have been awake such a long time." Her shoulders drooped and she hung her head forlornly. It was hard coping with her see-sawing emotions.

"Buck up, Em. Come and have some breakfast. That will fortify you for the task ahead. Toast, cereal, full English?" Graeme grinned teasingly. She caught the twinkle in his eyes.

"Mm! I suppose you're right," Emma reluctantly agreed, slipping out of her coat and sitting on the chair he so graciously pulled out for her.

"How can you be so cheerful?"

"Trust, Emma," he replied quietly.

Emma shook her head slowly in disbelief.

"You're spending the day with the Coopers, aren't you? So, I'm sure there'll be plenty of opportunity to speak with Doctor John and if you left half an hour earlier you'd be able to call in at the vicarage on the way and have a word with the Vicar."

As Emma sat reflecting on his words Graeme poured out a cup of tea, then, pushed the cereal packets towards her.

"Em, help yourself. I'll just take this up to Alex and collect Bethany. I can hear her stirring."

"I hope my rushing about hasn't disturbed her," she said apologetically.

"No, not at all, "Graeme assured her. "She's late waking this morning. I think it's all the excitement of yesterday; it really wore her out."

"She did enjoy opening her presents and playing with the toys, didn't she?"

"I think she found the empty boxes the most fun."

Emma nodded in agreement as a tear trickled unbidden down her cheek. They both smiled in remembrance, each thinking too, how much Mick and Val would have enjoyed the festivities with their granddaughter.

Much later, after an unhurried breakfast with her sister's family, Emma departed at a more reasonable time to off-load her burden of shame and seek forgiveness for her inappropriate behaviour on Christmas Eve from the Vicar and the Doctor.

She opened the front door of the Castleton home then stepped gingerly over the step to gain a foothold as a cold blast of air swirled around her. Snow was still in evidence on the gardens and along the lanes even though, the previous evening, Lord Edmund had instructed his estate manager to see that the access road leading to the main roads to Lowestoft and Norwich was unblocked and passable. Two of the lads had gone out with a tractor and trailer, one operating the snow plough attachment, creating a discernable track, whilst the other shovelled grit on to Main Street. Some householders had cleared their own garden paths as well as a walkway along the edge of their properties. Glad that she had on her boots, and was well wrapped up against the cold, Emma tentatively picked a route over the icy tracks and snowy drifts.

At the vicarage she was received with warmth and the twenty minutes or so she spent in the sanctuary of the Vicar's study, engaged in conversation and prayer, were a balm and a comfort to her grieving heart.

As she ventured out again, Emma trod carefully through the frozen drifts of snow blocking the lane to the Green, her heart still burdened with the words of apology she would use to express her contrition to Doctor John. So hard was she concentrating that she almost missed the childish voice that called out to her as she passed the Catton garden but Daniel's loud and insistent "Em! Emma!" eventually caught her attention. She paused by the gate and peered over the wall.

"Why, hello, Daniel. You look very busy. What have you there?" Emma asked.

"It's a snowman, of course," retorted the little boy.

Emma thoughtfully looked the mound of snow up and down, and then said, "A very fine one it is, too."

"Dad has gone in the house to get him a hat and I'm looking for something to make him some eyes and a nose."

"That must be very hard with all this snow covering the garden."

"Yes, I can't even find some stones," answered Daniel scraping ferociously at the ground with a trowel.

Emma pictured vegetables at the Stores that would have served Daniel's purpose so well; a carrot for a nose, nuts or tomatoes for eyes and she felt sure there was a curved courgette that would have made a beautiful smiley mouth. Daniel was getting fidgety.

"I'm not very good at helping you solve your problem, am I?"

Daniel looked hopefully at the bags Emma was carrying.

Emma smiled but slowly shook her head when she saw the direction of Daniel's eyes, "I'm afraid these are presents for the Doctor's family."

"Oh," he responded solemnly, disappointed not to have had a peek, just to see if there wasn't something that looked like a nose. Together they rooted around by the gate, he with his trowel on the garden side and she, with her feet, on the lane side. After a little while their disconsolate silence was broken by the opening of the front door. Adam came through carrying a hat and scarf. "Any success?" he called out to Daniel. Kirsten followed him clutching a paper bag.

"Look, Mummy's given me some biscuits."

"Oh, yummy."

"Not for you, silly; for the snowman. "

"Snowmen don't eat biscuits," said Daniel scornfully.

"They're to make his face," Kirsten declared emphatically and proceeded to press two ginger nuts into the firm snow head to represent eyes, a chocolate finger for his nose and two pink wafers for his mouth.

"Well done, Kirsty," complimented Adam. He handed the hat and scarf to Daniel, "Can you put these on him? I'm sure he'll look splendid."

As the children completed the decoration Adam came across the garden to speak with Emma.

"'Morning, Emma. How are you today?"

"Fine, now, thankyou."

"I'm really sorry about your loss…"

"Dad prayed for you at breakfast," butted in Daniel. "Em…ma?" he paused with his head to one side then, asked in a rush, "Why are you cross with God?"

Emma stared at him with a perplexed frown across her brow.

"'Cos her Mum and Dad's died, of course," said Kirsten in an exaggerated whisper to Daniel.

"But Dad said…"

"Shush!"

Emma looked across at Adam who raised his eyebrows heavenwards. "Out of the mouths of babes… etcetera!" He turned round to Daniel and Kirsten and said, "Go in and ask Mummy if we may have the camera to take a photo of you with this handsome fellow."

"Yippee!" yelled Daniel as they raced inside.

Adam looked with compassion and genuine concern at Emma. "We are praying for you and all the family that our Lord will help you bear the cross of grief which you are carrying at the moment. I fear Daniel has misunderstood my words and I have some explaining to do."

Tears welled up in Emma's eyes and a lump gathered in her throat. *Alex, you're right*, she thought, *people really do care*. She gulped rapidly then said, "We all truly appreciate your prayers, Adam. I believe it is the prayers of our friends that are enabling us to get through these days. Please don't stop. In fact, Daniel hit the nail on the head. When I first heard the news about Mum and Dad I was cross with God, and everyone else, very angry indeed. Stern words from my cousin, Justin, and the loving care of my family made me see the error of my behaviour. So, you see, I do need the believing prayers of you and Laura very much."

Adam placed his hand kindly on her shoulder.

"You have them, Emma," he assured her. "God go with you."

Emma smiled her thanks at Adam then waved goodbye to Daniel and Kirsten before continuing her trek to the Doctor's house, plodding valiantly through the snow that had built up at the end of the lane. Thoughtfully, as she crossed the Village Green, poignant memories jostled in her mind of the joyous evening, *Was it only two days ago?* which had been so rudely thwarted by the news of her parents fatal accident. She recalled the abandonment with which she had sung the familiar carols, surrounded by friends who were enjoying the fun and camaraderie of the occasion, the blizzard catching their breath and freezing their fingers and toes.

As she neared the Cooper's house Emma remembered the shock she felt at the sight of the missing Nicky, coming through the front door looking so frail and ill, followed by Josh Cook handcuffed to P.C. Prettyman. It was awful to see him frog-marched up the garden path by Sgt Catchpole to the waiting police vehicle. In her mind's eye Emma pictured her encounter with Roger Cooper just moments afterwards. She relived the surprise she felt at his changed demeanour towards herself. If she was really honest she had found that a startling and uncomfortable experience.

At the moment she felt the warm glow of anticipation that usually preceded a visit to the home of her friend, Jansy, it was a treasured childhood oasis, but coupled with it was uncertainty because she was overly anxious about seeing Roger again. She was dubious of his reaction to her and her response to him.

Thus, the last few steps were a strain emotionally, as well as physically, so that on arriving at the Cooper's house she all but tumbled through the front door as it was opened to receive her. Tears flooded her eyes as she was greeted with love into the heart of her friend's family.

Over the years Emma had always been made to feel welcome here and today was no exception. Trixie Cooper plied her with warming coffee whilst Doctor John brushed aside her halting apology with his usual affable graciousness. With the familiarity of long and deep friendship Jansy hugged her friend wordlessly but it spoke volumes to Emma's heart of her compassion and desire to come alongside her and share her grief.

In deference to Emma's feelings they planned to celebrate Jansy and Dave's engagement quietly but Emma made it clear that she didn't want it to be a sombre affair on her account. Dave was his usual quiet, serene self but it was impossible to stop Jansy's natural ebullience from spilling over. Her face was wreathed in smiles and both her eyes and conversation sparkled with joy.

Stephen, as lively as ever, had them in stitches with his never ending list of quips and jokes, then continued to regale the company, throughout dinner, with tales of his exploits on and off the football field. Trixie ensured that conversation flowed, remained light but not frivolous and John kept half a Doctor's eye on Emma. She was sat next to Roger but unsure how to handle his kind solicitous manner. Roger, too, was struggling to say the right thing knowing that in the past Emma's temper would flare up at the slightest provocation.

Trixie sensed their awkwardness with each other but was not really aware of the cause. She took opportunity as they rose from the table at the end of the meal to whisper, "Loosen-up, you two; it's like walking on eggshells. Just be yourselves." She put an arm around each of them affectionately.

"Off you go into the sitting room; catch up on all your news."

Emma made an attempt to clear the dining table but Trixie gently pulled her away and steered them both through the doorway.

"Stephen will help John deal with the dishes, while Jansy and Dave make coffee, so you two go and relax," Trixie smiled.

With that instruction they had no option but to smile back and comply.

They sat at opposite ends of the sofa. The silence stretched out between them, as taut as a kettle drum skin, till the Westminster clock on the mantelpiece chimed releasing the tension. Emma took the opportunity to furtively look across at Roger and found his deep blue eyes fixed on her. They were very penetrating, not threateningly so, but they certainly made her feel somewhat vulnerable. The depth of tenderness she saw displayed there caused her heart to miss a beat. She quickly looked away and fiddled with her fingers in her lap. For a young lady who was generally so articulate, self-assured and in control, Emma found the thoughts and emotions pervading her being at this time placed her at a serious disadvantage.

"You've changed," she ventured tentatively.

"So have you," came the gentle reply in that rich baritone voice that she loved. *Loved?* Whatever was she thinking about? How had that thought come unbidden into her mind? She felt her cheeks and neck burn and knew that she was uncontrollably blushing. Emma shook her head so that her auburn mane cascaded in front of her face partially hiding her embarrassment but not before Roger had seen the crimson glow so prettily enhance her features.

Cautiously he asked, "Em, whatever have I said to cause you such discomfort?"

Still with eyes cast down she shook her head and quickly said, "Nothing."

In that kindly tone Emma was reluctantly beginning to like, in preference to the disparaging tenor of voice she normally associated with him, Roger continued to enquire, "Does that mean you're having certain thoughts that cause you to blush so?"

Emma nodded warily.

"Would you care to share them?"

Her eyes flew to him and she shook her head vigorously.

They sat again in silence. Emma was uncomfortable as she struggled with these new inner emotions. Roger, however, was quite content to sit back, relaxed, arms folded and gaze at her uninterrupted, enjoying her loveliness.

After a while Emma peeped at him through a curtain of hair. Warmth exuded from the smile Roger gave her. Encouraged, she took the plunge and asked, "Why are you different?"

Roger's smile grew wider and reached his eyes. He leaned forward and readily explained.

"A new Pastor was appointed to the Church I have been attending in London, whilst at Med. School. He really caught my attention. Instead of just listening to the sermons he caused me to do some serious thinking. I really believed I was a Christian. I'd repented of my sins and accepted God's salvation through Jesus Christ some years ago but Pastor Johnson opened my eyes to see that I was living the Christian life according to the views of Roger D. Cooper. These were not necessarily Scripture based so with his guidance I've been studying the Word of God and attending Bible classes when I can. Under deep conviction of the Holy Spirit I came to realise that at times my attitude, behaviour and conversation were most un-Christ like." Roger paused as Emma shot bolt upright, pushed back her hair and focussed intently upon him. Almost imperceptibly she nodded and murmured, "Tell me about it!" reflecting on her own recent discovery and inner struggle on the Christian pathway but Roger took her words literally so continued.

"One Sunday Pastor Johnson directed our thoughts to Romans chapter twelve, particularly Paul's words in verse three, "Let God transform you inwardly by a complete change of your mind. Then you will be able to know the will of God, what is good and pleasing to Him and is perfect." This had such an impact on me. I prayed for guidance to think and act God's way. I surrendered completely to the Lord, stopped thinking so selfishly and learned not only to talk with Him but also to listen to His voice. At this moment in time I seek His will for my life through prayer, Bible reading and trust. He is now in control and we share a very precious intimacy. I'm different, Emma, because of Him."

Emma looked across at him through the tears that had gathered in her eyes and spoke hesitantly, "Oh, Roger, I didn't..." She broke off as Jansy burst into the room.

"Here we are," Jansy declared cheerfully, holding open the door for Dave to carry through the coffee tray.

Roger caught Emma's eye and leaning forwards, lightly touched her arm, and said quietly, "Can we finish this conversation later?"

Emma nodded, quickly composed her features and looked up at Jansy with a set smile upon her lips that didn't reach her eyes as she accepted the mug of coffee Jansy handed to her. Roger's stomach churned over as he watched Emma steel her countenance to respond to Jansy's anxious enquiry, "How you doing, Em?"

"Sometimes I'm fine, Jans, but at other times it's an effort to stay calm and composed," Emma confided to her friend as Jansy sat down beside her on the sofa.

"It's not surprising. The accident has been a shock to us all," Jansy replied, unsure how to answer the young woman who hitherto had been self-sufficient, always in control, but who, in Jansy's eyes, seemed to be floundering and at breaking point.

"It's hard to trust in a God who allows such an awful thing to happen," Emma continued. "When I'm with Alex and Graeme, or Justin and Aunt Bernice and Uncle Roy, their positive attitude carries me along. But, when I'm alone my feelings fluctuate between confident hope and deep despair. I feel so crushed by the heaviness in my heart that, at times, I can't seem to find God at all."

"Dear Em, I'm so sorry," said Jansy thickly, a sob in her throat as she affectionately held Emma's arm.

Doctor John, who, with Trixie, had come to join the young people for coffee, recognised his daughter was struggling with her emotions, joined in the conversation.

"I think you're wise, Emma, to keep company with those who help you cope with this situation rather than staying on your own. We all touch one another's hearts. Even though your heart is broken, Emma, you'll find God is right there. Talk to Him. Tell Him how you feel. He is listening. Allow your faith to lift your feelings."

Emma shook her head disbelievingly.

Gently, John continued, "Have you read His Word, Emma? Have you let Him speak His words of comfort to your heart?"

Again, Emma shook her head and said with a sigh, "I don't know where to look. Justin and Graeme keep quoting verses of Scripture to me but I struggle to find them in my Bible."

"I'm sure if you could only read them for yourself, Em, you would gain considerable comfort and help," Trixie encouragingly affirmed.

Roger, who had been listening to this exchange, asked thoughtfully, "Emma, would you like me to write down some key verses for you?"

Clutching at the life-line being offered her Emma replied with longing in her voice and pleading in her eyes, "Yes please, Roger."

"Do you know, Emma, when we pray for and love one another in Christ's name it's sometimes necessary to ask for specific help if a need is to be met?" queried John.

"Yes, I suppose you're right," she reluctantly agreed.

"Emma, don't be too proud to ask. We all want to help you through this difficult time," encouraged John sensitively.

"Thankyou, Doctor," Emma murmured gratefully. "I would be glad if you would pray for me."

"Now?"

"Yes," she answered without hesitation.

In his own indomitable, yet warm-hearted style, John drew them all together in the way he stood up, held out his hands, closed his eyes and focussed on his Lord as he prepared his heart and mind to intercede for Emma. Trixie took hold of Emma's hand and grasped the one John outstretched towards her. The others promptly stood to join them, linking hands to form an unbroken circle of prayer, as the Doctor voiced his petition.

After their impromptu prayer session there followed a delightful time of sharing and exchange of presents. Emma's demeanour appeared noticeably changed, an aura of tranquillity permeating her conversation and behaviour. Time flew as they enjoyed each other's company. About an hour or so later, Stephen in fine humour left the group chatting about Jansy and Dave's plans for the future as well as discussing possible options open to Emma, in view of her parent's death, after she graduated later in the New Year.

Stephen's long strides enabled him to cover the icy terrain more quickly than Emma had done earlier in the day. He soon reached the Andaman's cottage where conversation centred on the supposed crimes Josh Cook had been apprehended for.

"I did hear that stuff was missing from Miss Pedwardine's hamper when it was delivered," said Rosalie.

"That's hard to believe, Uncle Mick was so meticulous," commented Stephen.

"You're right," confirmed Nicky. "He was a stickler for precision and correctness. I was in real trouble once for not placing the orders in the exact position in the van. Did I know about it!"

"Who delivered it?" asked Annette.

"Apparently Josh."

"But why take anything out of it?"

"He says for his Mum."

"That doesn't make sense. Mrs Darnell took them a huge Christmas Hamper from the Church."

"Perhaps he didn't know."

"May be, but what about the break-in at the Manor?"

"I think that's the reason I got clobbered," said Nicky reflectively.

"Whatever do you mean?" Melvin demanded sharply.

"We...ll! Josh has been attempting to cadge a lift with me for weeks, when I make deliveries to Lord Edmund, but each time I fobbed him off because I suspected he had ulterior motives. He's been trying to get me involved in his exploits for ages; he's always boasting about his skills at fooling people; how easy it is. He got real annoyed with me when I wouldn't go along with it."

"Oh, Nicky," sighed Annette, "why didn't you share? We could have prayed about it."

"Sorry, Annie, but I did my best to steer him away from dishonest ways and get him involved in the Church programme. Although he frequently came to youth club and house group nothing seemed to touch his heart. He was blatantly arrogant. It was almost as if he was challenging God and every time a crime paid off he was one up on God," said Nicky despondently.

"Well, mate," said Stephen with encouraging gusto, as he slapped his friend on the back, "no one could have tried harder than you." Nicky flinched.

"But I feel as though I failed him."

"No, son, Josh made his own choices," reminded Melvin.

"I shall never forget the look of disbelief on his face when he walked into our house and saw you there," Stephen said.

"Until that moment I couldn't believe he would callously clobber a mate but his reaction gave him away," Nicky reflected sadly.

"I agree, in fact, I'm flabbergasted to learn that Josh behaved so cold-heartedly to a friend. You said Nicky's attacker might turn out to be someone we knew, Stephen. At the time I didn't believe you. I also think, if it's true, his treatment of Mrs Jenner was exceptionally cruel," said tender-hearted Annette. "How did he think she would manage to live without her pension?"

"I don't suppose he gave any thought to that aspect of his actions; he'd conned her out of her pension card and tricked Alex Castleton into giving him Mrs Jenner's money. That was his triumph; didn't matter if any one suffered. He'd won."

"That was dire enough but the attack on Mrs Darnell was outrageous!"

"Yet not as outrageous as their possible involvement in the Kemp's accident."

"What do you mean, Stephen?"

"Well, as you know the police were at our house yesterday, and I overheard conversations, between Sgt Catchpole and Dan Prettyman, following phone calls from Northumbrian police. These suggested the Cooks were somehow implicated, though I don't know any details." As Stephen finished imparting this dreadful news four pairs of horrified eyes were turned towards him.

"Oh, no," gasped Rosalie quite distressed. "That poor, poor woman, however will she survive such a shocking blow? You say they think both Joe and Josh are involved? Oh, dear! Joe's misdeeds have caused her so much worry in recent years. She's a waif of the woman she was. A breath of wind will knock her over. If true, this news will surely finish Michelle. Dear God, be her strength," she whispered fervently.

Following this disclosure, amazingly within a short space of time, the news spread throughout the village community. Soon, speculation was rife concerning Joe and Josh Cook's likely involvement in the spate of incidents in the area over recent weeks.

It was not often that anything occurred to shake the villagers from the wintry doldrums that descended after the last holiday makers returned home. In fact, they were usually glad of the respite and slipped into sleepy hibernatory oblivion that winter months offered to them, absorbing the peace and quiet after the summer's busyness. However, these incidents awakened them early, stimulated diverse theories and caused much guesswork to be bandied about in most homes within the village.

CHAPTER ELEVEN

$\Large{}$ For most of the Newton Westerby residents Christmas soon became a faint memory, the following days assuming their usual routine, but for Alex and Emma this was not possible. The loss of their parents left a huge gap in their working life as well as their family life. So, there was no return to normality for them because Mick and Val were not there to fulfil their vital roles. Both young women recognised adjustments would have to be made, but deciding what they were to be proved difficult.

Emma was adamant she was returning to College to complete her course, "after the week is out," and equally determined she was not ever going to work in a shop where "people thieve and bicker! I'm not a pushover like my father!" she declared on Boxing Day evening. Roger Cooper had walked with her to Alex and Graeme's home, stayed for tea, and shared in the discussion on the future of the Village Stores.

"Oh, Em!" said Alex with feeling, "Dad behaved towards people as he did because he cared about them. He didn't see them just as customers but rather as fellow children of God with needs. Sometimes they were of a practical nature and at other times they were of a spiritual sort. In each instance he did his utmost to point them in the right direction, either to the proper shelf in the shop or the relevant passage in the Bible. You know that was Dad's way."

"Yeah! And how many times was he taken advantage of?" scoffed Emma irritably.

Alex caught Graeme's eye and sighed with a heavy heart. Why did Emma have to be so difficult?

Fortunately, their brother, Drew telephoned partway through the conversation. Calmly, he suggested to his sisters that they keep faith with the villagers and adhere to their father's plans for the shop's opening hours over the holiday period. "We'll discuss any long term proposals for the shop when Morag and I fly down from Edinburgh for the funeral." Alex and Emma gratefully agreed to his recommendation.

Throughout the ensuing days their hearts were warmed yet again by the way the villagers rallied around them. The Village Stores and Post Office re-opened according to Mick's schedule with help from Rosalie, Christina and Pauline who, despite their own busy lives and commitments, graciously formulated a rota. This ensured that not only were opening hours covered but also, the behind the scenes everyday tasks of running a shop, were attended to. This was easier said than done for Val and Mick were masters at their trade and their expertise was sorely missed in more ways than one; none more so than Val's ready meals-for-one, as Mr Bracewell vociferously pointed out, "'ere ye ent got m'dinners!"

"No, Mr Bracewell," said Rosalie patiently.

"Well, ye'd best be quick abaht it, I in't gor'all day."

"Shu'rup, yew blitherin' ole fewell," interspersed Mrs Saunders, who was next in the queue, "there won't be none will there' wi' Val bein' dead? Choose summat else, my man, like us all" Her blunt manner pulled Mr Bracewell up with a start. The penny dropped!

"Yew mean…?"

Mrs Saunders nodded.

"Won't be noo more."

He shuffled towards the freezer, pausing at the delicatessen counter on the way. "Noo pies, neither?"

"No, Mr Bracewell," said Rosalie quietly.

"It's a good job them Kemp girls aren't in the shop to 'ear yew a goin' on," scolded Mrs Saunders.

This upsetting scenario was just one of many similar ones that morning. The glum looks on the faces of the other customers added to the despondent snatches of conversation Rosalie overheard as she served the old gentleman.

"Over the years we've depended on Val's baking."

"Yes, we've taken it for granted for such a long time," said another.

"She was a brilliant good cook. We'll miss her so."

"Oh dear, what are we gooin' tew dew?" lamented Mrs Jenner, repeatedly wringing her hands.

As she continued to serve the customers, Rosalie's throat caught with choked-up emotion. Countless thoughts flew around in her head. *However are we going to satisfy the customer's demands? I hope the girls come up with a solution. I can bake to please my family but not to Val's standard and certainly not the proliferation or assortment of choice that people are used to.* Steak and kidney pie was Rosalie's speciality and she was going to keep to that. She occasionally experimented, mostly for Annette's veggie dishes, but generally she stuck to the same mundane, traditional meals the family enjoyed. No, she wasn't the one to take on the insatiable appetite of the village and its visitors looking for more exotic fare.

Later that morning, Michelle Cook came in, with Bradley and Thomas, to pick up some milk and look for any special offers on the reduced-price shelf.

Alex and Emma had already spoken with Rosalie, Christina and Pauline about what they should do if Michelle came into the shop.

"We really can't refuse to serve her. It would make things very difficult for her. Where else would she get the basic essentials and cheap food to feed her family if she was denied service here?"

"In all conscience I'm not willing to serve her."

"I know she doesn't drive and she can't afford the bus fare to town but I truly can't serve her."

"It's very un-Christian behaving like this; after all, Michelle isn't responsible for Joe and Josh's actions."

"The Vicar wouldn't approve if we refused to deal with Michelle. I can't forget his words after Mrs Darnell was found beaten up. His Christmas sermon is still vivid in my mind, "Father forgive.""

"I would find it hard to attend to her, after what happened to Nicky, but I would do it," said Rosalie gravely.

"I'd give 'er a piece o' my mind," declared Christina gruffly.

Ever the diplomat Pauline said, "We're only across the road, so, any problems, Billy or I will come and serve."

"It's alright for yew; none o' yow'n was hurt," muttered Christina.

Now Michelle was here. Rosalie was on her own. She took a deep breath, whispered a prayer and put on a smile. With an effort to remain impartial she said, "Good morning," as pleasantly as she could.

Michelle didn't utter a word but sheepishly put the wire basket on the counter. In the background, two loud-mouthed women from Marsh Newton were talking pointedly in exaggerated stage whispers about the alleged misdemeanours of Josh and his father. Michelle packed her bag, paid her money and ushered her boys out of the shop pretty sharpish without a backward glance. Rosalie breathed a sigh of relief that all passed without further incident. The remarks of the women had been cruel and scathing; Michelle couldn't fail to have heard them. Yet, it had probably taken a great deal of courage for her to come into the shop at all; the needs of her children overriding any personal feelings.

On the day of Val and Mick's funeral the Village Stores and the Post Office were closed all day but, surprisingly, no one was heard to complain. Rather, the villagers turned out in force to support the family, packing the Church with their bodies and uniting their voices in an affirmation of positive faith.

Afterwards, as the family gathered at the graveside, the Women's Guild, who had so graciously offered to attend to refreshments, hastily set out extra plates and cups and saucers.

Graeme Castleton, realising the unexpected influx of people might cause the ladies embarrassment, had slipped the store key into Rosalie Andaman's hand as he passed her, on leaving the Church, and quietly suggested, "Help yourself to whatever is needed to make up the shortfall; biscuits, milk, rolls, fillings, you know." Rosalie nodded.

Throughout the day Emma's thoughts were in turmoil. She was no longer angry about her parent's accident and her heart was at peace concerning their eternity. In spite of that, she was still battling with her emotions regarding Roger Cooper, her conscience with regard to the future of the Stores and her dreams involving a possible redirection of career.

Every word spoken by the Vicar in the service had received an assenting echo from her heart, however, just one phrase lingered on in her mind, "Live a life worthy of the Lord, please Him in every way," which Hugh quoted from Colossians 1 v 10. He had mentioned the exemplary life of her parents and pointed out that "they are not now in heaven because of any goodness or kindness they have shown to people but because they believed in the work of Jesus Christ upon the cross and accepted Him as Saviour. Their place in heaven is assured because they knew they were forgiven. The redemption they experienced enabled them to live lives worthy of the Lord. The fragrance of Jesus touched every aspect of their lives so that above all else they wanted their daily living to honour and please Him in every way. Those of you who knew them best know this to be true."

Hugh challenged the congregation, "Are you living lives worthy of the Lord? Are you pleasing Him in every way? Not just in attitude and behaviour, but conversation and thoughts, decisions and actions. If their passing causes us to give the Lord His rightful place in our lives, pleasing Him in every way, it will not have been in vain. Our reason for living is to glorify God. Are you...?"

Am I, considered Emma, *living a life pleasing to Him, I mean?* This question tossed over and over in her mind. She couldn't let it go. *I know I'm wilful; I like my own way. I think I'm always right. I don't appreciate having my plans frustrated… a life pleasing to Him … pleasing, honouring, glorifying; putting Him first. Uhmm!* She reflected, *not me and what I want, or what I think I want, pleasing Him. Gosh, this is tough!*

Discerning as ever, Aunt Bernice noticed Emma's distraction, had a quiet word with Justin and Roger as they stood talking, whilst collecting their cups of tea after the committal, then steered Emma in their direction. She knew they would shield her from idle village gossip and be perceptive to her needs, physical as well as spiritual.

Afterwards, Emma could remember very little about standing in the cemetery or the time spent in the Church hall following the funeral service or, in fact, how she had arrived at Green Pastures, Aunt Bernice and Uncle Roy's home, that evening. Since the service she had felt cocooned in a bubble of unreality trying to sort out Hugh Darnell's challenging words for herself; *Live worthily, pleasing the Lord.* They were God's words directly to her and she could no longer dismiss them as irrelevant to her life. She'd done that for far too long.

"Walk worthy of the …"

"What did you say?" Emma shouted sharply, almost accusingly, at Justin and Drew, who were standing closest to her.

The cacophony of conversation around her had not impacted upon Emma's solitude; it had taken that phrase to penetrate the wall of deep thought that had engulfed her all day.

Drew moved forward and took hold of his sister's hands. Looking into her startled face he briefly explained the discussion that had been taking place, of which, Emma was totally unaware.

"Em, we've been talking about the future of the shop and the bungalow. We've looked at the possibility of closure and

considered the consequences if we do so. I've had someone
in to do a valuation. By selling the business and the three
properties we would each be very well off financially. Just think
of that, Em; you could be very affluent indeed. How does that
appeal to you?"

Emma gave him such an odd look that Drew rapidly
continued. "In some ways, for us, that would be the easiest
option but, it has been pointed out, disastrous for this
community. Morag and I offered to sell up the dentist practice
and move down here to run the shop if Alex will keep the Post
Office going but, we love our life in Edinburgh, so don't really
want to go down that route if we can find an acceptable
alternative.

"Oh no, you can't do that."

"Yes, that's what Uncle Roy was just saying. If we were
to do so, the people covered by the practice would be deprived
of a dental service and that doesn't seem right either."

"Certainly not," agreed Morag, emphatically.

"Justin was reminding us that we each need to walk worthy
of the vocation to which we have been called, whether it's
as dentist, builder, accountant or teacher. To fulfil that calling
faithfully, and not assume responsibility for someone else's
calling, should be our intent."

"Yes I think so, too."

"You do?"

"In fact, I've been doing a lot of thinking, today."

"You have?"

Emma looked round at the smiling faces. They were not
mocking her but anxious and supportive. She turned her eyes
slowly upon each one; dear Aunt Bernice and Uncle Roy,
behind Drew was Morag and on the other side of her was Alex
and Graeme with Justin, and across the room sitting on the
sofa, she could see the Vicar and Mrs Darnell.

"Where's Bethany?"

"Jacky's babysitting and Doctor and Mrs Cooper are staying
in with Ellie and Gareth." Emma nodded with understanding.

"No Uncle Gordon and Aunt Cynthia?" She glanced enquiringly at Roy.

"No, my dear," he replied "you know Gordon as well as I; he does tend to view things negatively and put a damper on proceedings."

"Gordon was annoyed he and Cynthia were not invited, commenting that "after all Val was my sister too,"" elaborated Bernice "but Ben, bless the dear boy, as usual calmed his father down and told him this evening get together was not about Val, but you and Alex and the future of the Stores."

"Oh! I see!" Emma glanced at her sister. "Roger?" she asked quietly. Alex shook her head slowly in response.

Moving towards her sister Emma said, "Alex, you're not going to sell the Stores, are you? I don't think Dad would be very pleased if we did that."

"It was mentioned in passing but I don't really think it is an option. Like you, I feel it would be letting Mum and Dad down if we don't attempt to keep the Stores going, nevertheless, we do have a number of practical issues to sort out."

"Such as?"

"Oh Em! Just about everything. You know Mum and Dad did virtually the whole lot; Rosalie served in the shop, Nicky did Saturday deliveries and you and I helped out as and when we could but, the bulk of the everyday running of the shop was in their hands, responsibility on their shoulders."

"That's all very airy-fairy, Alex. I should have thought with your methodical brain you would have made an itemised list of what needs doing and who is available to do it."

"We haven't got down to specifics, Em," said Drew sensing that Alex was taken aback by Emma's forthrightness and Graeme was preparing to rise in his wife's defence.

"Selling the property sounds very specific to me," retorted Emma angrily "where do you propose we live? Out on the Common?"

Seeking to diffuse the fraught situation, Bernice innocently asked, "What would you suggest, Emma dear?"

Without further preamble Emma proceeded to elaborate, and voice the schemes, that had been formulating in her mind throughout the day.

"Well, I certainly wouldn't sell anything and put everyone on the street!" She looked meaningfully at her brother. "I think Alex and Graeme should move into the bungalow, more space, fantastic garden; their cottage would make a super gallery and studio with that gorgeous upstairs window. I truly would like to finish my course and qualify to teach. That's only another term. Then, I'll put my career on hold and run the Stores, if Alex will be responsible for the Post Office and the accounts."

They all gasped as she paused for breath.

However, without giving anyone else the opportunity to speak Emma continued, "I know it's a complete U-turn on my part but I've been thinking all day about your words, Vicar, and I really do want to live my life in a way that is pleasing to the Lord. In my view taking responsibility for the shop and attending to the needs of other people instead of pleasing myself, boosting my own ego by opening my own art gallery and teaching studio, would be the better option at this moment in time.

"I've given this matter considerable thought and prayer today. I have incredible peace about it. I feel that by serving this community, as Mum and Dad did, I can honour God and share my faith in a practical way.

"I know I can't cook, but I can clean and work hard, and I'd welcome the challenge of doing the window displays. I spent a lot of time working alongside Dad so I think I could do the orders and deal with the suppliers.

"Mum always drummed into me health and safety issues, sell by dates etc.; I shall never forget, they were almost her last words to me," Emma paused, faltering for a moment then, drew a deep breath and continued, "and I've learned the knack of dealing with awkward customers by observing Mum and Dad's tactics and watching Rosalie but I still can't bake."

"Mmm! That is a sticking point!" commented Drew sarcastically.

"Freshly baked foods and the frozen and fresh meals that were Mum's speciality are the big draw to customers, locals as well as holiday makers. How do you aim to solve that problem?" Alex enquired.

Emma's eyes lit up. "I'm still working on it but I don't think it's insurmountable," she replied confidently, "for instance, it might be worth talking to Tessa Jenner, who's very much into organic and veggie dishes, also cousin Jilly over at Newton Lokesby is…" Emma spent the rest of the evening enthusiastically regaling her family with some of the ideas she had for continuing, or even expanding her parents' work. They were astonished at some of her suggestions but could also see the careful thought she had given to ensure her proposals were workable.

"Em, don't forget we still have the threat of closure from the Post Office bosses to contend with," pointed out Alex quietly, not wishing to dampen Emma's initiative but very much aware of the devastation threatened culling plans, announced for rural post offices, could have for them and the villages they served.

"I'll fight tooth and nail to keep this very necessary facility open for our community. Dad wouldn't give in and neither shall I." Emma replied defiantly. "It's not just about stamps and benefits but providing the services our community needs."

Roy smiled at his niece, detecting in her the spirit and passion of both her parents. "I admire your spunk, my girl. We'll do all we can to support you."

Emma returned his smile. "Thanks, Uncle Roy," she said gratefully.

As the evening drew to a close there were still some imponderables that required answers. Should Alex and Graeme move into the bungalow? If so, what were they to do about their cottage? Rent or sell? Did Emma want to stay in the flat over the Stores or would she like to move into the cottage?

Would it ever be suitable as Em's art gallery? Should Drew and Morag come home? Sell up or close the shop? Could they approach the situation positively in view of the bureaucratic axe aimed at their livelihood or should they build for the future on some of Emma's ideas? There was much indecision concerning the right direction for them all.

Emma was very perplexed by Drew's attitude, particularly when he suddenly produced documents that he wanted Alex and her to sign giving him sovereignty over the business and their homes. Instantly, Alex felt a considerable amount of unease and sensed antagonism rising in Emma. With pleading in her eyes, she looked up at Graeme who, with care, suggested they leave it a day or two, in order to give it more thought. Reluctantly Drew acquiesced.

Disquiet pervaded the air. Sensitive to the feelings of all concerned, Rev Hugh rose solemnly from his seat; he and Penny were there to give balanced and unbiased counsel so, bringing the gathering to an end Hugh prayed for the people involved and their problems concluding, "Father God, You hold each one in Your heart; guide, direct and control the way they should go. In Your name and for Your sake, we pray. Amen."

CHAPTER TWELVE

The next morning a wintry sun appeared in the sky and the thaw began. Emma decided it was time to return home to her flat. She had appreciated the support and companionship of Alex and Graeme during the difficult days following their parents' death but she didn't want to outstay her welcome. The challenge of life without Val and Mick had to be faced.

Also, she felt she ought to tackle her outstanding College assignments as well as apply energy and thought into the running of the Village Stores if the family were to take seriously her declaration of responsibility.

So, she dropped off her overnight bag, adjusted the setting on the central heating, as the flat felt rather cold, and then ran down the back stairs to the corridor that led into the shop. As she neared the bottom step her stomach suddenly churned over.

"Ooh!" she gasped as she remembered the last time she had come down this way. Her Dad had stood at the bottom, mischief in his eyes, playfully wishing her a Happy Christmas Eve. Emma slowed down; her eyes puddled with tears. She took a deep breath, prayed for strength, then with head held high opened the door which led into the back storeroom.

Rosalie, who was stacking tins on to a shelf turned round, surprised at seeing Emma walk into the shop. She sensed a certain vulnerability in the young woman before her and greeted her warmly with a smile.

"Why, Emma, good morning. I am pleased to see you." She paused in her task.

"Hi, Rosalie, not busy?"

"We had a rush early on but, now there's a quiet spell so, I'm making the most of it by filling up empty shelves." Rosalie put down the can in her hand, looked up at Emma, whose angular form towered above her, so similar to her father, and said, "Emma, we haven't done the end of month stock-take and we're running low on some items. I know it's not going to be easy for you but would it be possible for us to do it together and place the necessary orders?"

Rosalie's direct common-sense manner put Emma at ease and enabled her to approach the matter in a business like way.

"Yes, I'd appreciate your help, Rosalie. You're probably more aware of what we need than I am at the moment. As you know Alex is tied up sorting through Mum and Dad's things in the bungalow, with Drew and Morag, but we're hoping to get back into some sort of routine by next week. So, for the present it's just you and me. How long do you think it will take us?"

"We…ell! It all depends," Rosalie began haltingly.

"On how quick I am on the uptake?" quipped Emma with a grin.

"No, I didn't mean that; though at first we might not be as efficient as your Dad. After years of experience, he had everything at his fingertips. It really depends on when we decide to do it and how many customers we have interrupting us."

"Oh, yes, I see what you mean," Emma was thoughtful for a moment. "It's important, then, that we stock-take ASAP?"

"Yes, it is."

"Right! We'll start at half-past ten, look at the paperwork in the office over coffee, and then work till half-past twelve. Will that be OK Rosalie? I do need you to show me the ropes, please. I may not do things exactly like Dad. We'll need to work out our own system. See what works best for us."

Rosalie slowly nodded her agreement then said, "We can't both be shut in the office and leave the shop unattended, though."

"No, I didn't intend that. Aunt Bernice has offered help whenever we need a hand. I'll go now and call her," and Emma walked to the office to do just that.

"Oh!" exclaimed Rosalie dubiously, unaware of the magnificent way Bernice Durrant had marshalled the customers Christmas Eve morning when Nicky had gone missing and she wasn't in the shop. Rosalie finished stacking the shelf she was working on then went to serve Mrs Jenner who was waiting at the till.

"How are you today?" Rosalie enquired of the old lady.

"Well, my dear, much, much better since Doctor Cooper, Sgt Tom and the dear Vicar sorted everything out for me. Can't think how I let that nasty boy talk me out of my pension card and 'e never give me a penny, not a penny. I won't never try 'n taak things from the shop again. Now what did I 'ave? I mus' pay yew for 'em." She fumbled in her bag for her purse.

"Mrs Jenner," said Rosalie firmly, "you don't owe the shop anything. You just need to pay for today's groceries," but Mrs Jenner wasn't listening, she was busy reckoning up.

"I took a tin of tuna, a loaf and some..." The bell on the shop door jangled. Rosalie glanced up and saw it was Roger Cooper.

"Emma?" he enquired.

Rosalie smiled and replied, "In the office."

He walked in the direction she pointed. Rosalie turned back to deal with Mrs Jenner who was still reiterating her list "... beans, a box of eggs and a potato and carr..."

"Mrs Jenner," Rosalie raised her voice in order to catch the attention of the distracted old lady, "those groceries were your Christmas present from the Village Stores." She proceeded to take the items from the wire basket on the counter and ring them through the till. "That will be £3.76p, please."

"Is that all? I'm sure it's more than that." Mrs Jenner pulled out a £10 note and thrust it at Rosalie. "'ere taak that."

Patiently, Rosalie waited for Mrs Jenner to put some items into her shopping bag, stop flapping about and then said, "Mrs Jenner, please listen."

Pausing in her packing Mrs Jenner looked up at Rosalie.

"This is your receipt for today's shopping and your change. You owe nothing for the groceries you had for Christmas. They are taken care of."

"Oh, my dear, how kind."

As Mrs Jenner doddered out of the door still murmuring to herself, "how very kind," Rosalie heard discontented mutterings from customers down one of the aisles.

"Seems it pays to shoplift."

"P'rhaps we ought to try it, eh?"

Rosalie raised her voice deliberately to let them know she had overheard them, "mitigating circumstances."

"Oh, yeah!" retorted one disbelievingly.

Meanwhile, in the office, Emma duly rang Aunt Bernice, who was pleased to be asked to "hold the fort" as she put it and agreed to come to the shop straightaway. Whilst she was speaking on the phone Emma heard a tap on the door and was delighted to see it was Roger, when he poked his head around the door. She inclined her head to acknowledge his wave but after a moment he withdrew, to enable her to complete her business in private.

After the call to her Aunt, Emma telephoned Tessa Jenner, who arranged to arrive at the shop about half-past two that afternoon to chat over Emma's proposals with regard to organic supplies. Emma also phoned her non-working-chef cousin, Jilly Briggs, and persuaded her to meet that evening to discuss future catering provision for the Village Stores.

Satisfied with the outcome of her efforts Emma locked the office, anxious to share them with Rosalie, and eager to chat with Roger. In vain she looked up and down the aisles for him but she only spotted her assistant, standing by the display barrow, talking to Laura Catton. As Emma approached them she heard Laura enquire about the cakes and trifles that had been ordered for the New Year Party, for village children, which the Vicar's wife usually organized.

"'Morning, Laura."

"Hi, Emma. Just checking on the food for the annual children's bash. I'm helping out because of Mrs Darnell's accident."

"No problem. We have it all in hand. Let Rosalie know your precise requirements. Will you collect or do you want it delivered?"

"Oh, someone will collect the order, early afternoon, thanks," said Laura gratefully.

"You're welcome," Emma smiled then turned to greet other customers, among them Jansy Cooper, who had called in for bread and milk for her mother. She instantly clasped Emma's arm and whispered, "June, if we can find somewhere to live. You will be my bridesmaid, won't you?"

"I'd be delighted, Jans," Emma replied softly, looking either side of her friend. "Did Roger come in with you?"

Jansy chuckled "Of course not, he trusts me out on my own, now. I am a big girl."

As the other shoppers clustered around the two friends, admiring Jansy's ring and subtly pumping her about a wedding date, Rosalie, with considerable misgivings, made a note of the number of cakes and trifles required for the children's party, wondering how on earth they were going to fulfil the order without Val. She glanced across at Emma, who appeared quite unperturbed. It would be some while before she learned the gist of Emma's telephone conversations with possible solutions to this very real dilemma.

Soon afterwards, Laura and her children left the Stores, but once outside she was overcome with dizziness. She sat down on the bench and sent Daniel to ask Rosalie for a glass of water. Both Emma and Rosalie dashed outside to check on Laura, leaving the shop unattended. A knot of people huddled inquisitively by the shop door. The thaw had set in, rapidly melting the snow and ice that had lingered since Christmas Eve.

"I think I must have slipped," explained Laura. "I'll be alright in a few minutes," she assured those who were hovering close to her, not wishing to be too much bother to anyone.

"Are you sure? I can take you home in the van," offered Emma.

"Thanks, Emma, but we'll manage."

"I'll walk with yew, Mrs Catton, while Mum's in the shop," suggested Ryan Saunders. Mrs Saunders nodded and pushed her son forwards.

"Thankyou, Ryan." Emma caught Rosalie's arm and drew her to one side. "How did Dad deal with this mess?" she asked quietly, indicating the slush that was being traipsed into the store.

"If Laura's alright, I'll sort it out."

Laura nodded her assent.

"Thanks." Emma returned through the shop door, taking care not to slip herself, in time to see Mr Bracewell stuffing produce into his pockets and a woman from the Common loading her shopping bag with tins.

Oh, dear! Lord, please, keep me calm. Help me to handle this, she quietly prayed, then walked straight up to the culprits, smiled and held out her hands.

"Mr Bracewell, I'm so sorry there was no one here to assist you. Mrs Catton was taken poorly just as she left the shop but I'm here now so I'll weigh your things first, then I'll attend to Mrs Gooch who hasn't been able to find a wire basket for her shopping."

Presenting an unruffled front, Emma, dealt with the erring customers. Mr Bracewell had the grace to look shame-faced at what he had tried to do but Mrs Gooch was quite miffed at being found out. So, she remained silent, particularly as Mrs Saunders and some loud-mouthed women, from Marsh Newton came in, quickly followed by Aunt Bernice.

"See yew're running out," one remarked spitefully, indicating an empty shelf.

"Not too fresh, neither," observed another, turning over the carrots.

"When yew closing down?"

"Soon by the looks of things," called a disgusted voice.

"All thanks to them dratted Cooks." spat out someone else.

"Now, now ladies that will do," said Aunt Bernice, having heard most of this exchange as she entered the shop and before she had opportunity to remove her coat. "There is, unfortunately, always a lull in supplies when Christmas and New Year fall on a Friday; difficulty with deliveries because of holidays, but I do assure you, new provisions will be in next week."

"Uhm!" they grunted in disbelief.

"Just bear with us. You're all aware of the circumstances," Bernice paused and looked directly at each of them, meaningfully.

"In the meantime," she clapped her hands as she bustled over to the fresh veg stand and commenced filling a brown paper bag with a selection of vegetables, "we have a special New Year offer, veggie stew packs for 50p, while stocks last; go well with the meat packs on offer at the butchers." Bernice nodded towards Billy Cooper's shop across the road from the Stores, glad she'd looked in the window as she passed, albeit briefly.

Emma looked across at a startled Rosalie and mouthed, "Quick thinking!" She walked briskly to cover the distance between them, took her assistant's arm, and steered her towards the office. Once the door was closed Emma said, "Aunt Bernice is in her element."

"But…"

"What would Dad have done?"

"Well…!"

"Customer relations! Customer relations, every time," said Emma with a twinkle in her eye.

"Yes, but…"

"Handling people is Aunt Bernice's forte and we won't have any waste!"

Rosalie smiled. "You're a chip off the old block, Emma. The Stores will do well with you in charge."

"No, we'll work together. You've far more experience than me. At the moment I've just got ideas. Working in partnership we'll make it succeed."

Over coffee Emma shared her vision and then, they pored over Mick's suppliers files, checked the stock and compiled the list for Cash and Carry the next day. On the phone she placed orders, spoke to her brother and contacted the ladies on her Mother's baking team, to enquire what they were still willing to do. On the whole their time together was constructive and both Emma and Rosalie were encouraged when at twenty minutes to one they left the office to see how Aunt Bernice had fared in the Stores.

"Oh, Emma! I've had such a marvellous time. Thankyou for asking me. Anytime, I'll be glad to help." Bernice grabbed Emma's hands, "I hope I did right with those grumblers."

"You did just fine. I'm proud of you, Aunt Bernice," Emma hugged her Aunt affectionately.

"Could you come in tomorrow? Same time? Drew is taking me to Cash and Carry. I have to register as a signatory. Alex will too, but tomorrow she and Morag plan to complete sorting the bungalow. In future, we're hoping it will be possible for Nicky to pick up the order if Alex or I fax it through first."

"Of course, dear."

"Well, then, I'll have to put you on the pay roll."

"Don't be silly, dear. I'm family. I'm just helping out."

Emma caught Rosalie's eye. "Pay. That's something else we didn't discuss, though I think that might be Alex's department."

Rosalie nodded and murmured, "Probably."

Promptly at half-past two, Tessa Jenner, pulled up in her people carrier and parked outside the Village Stores. She swept majestically through the shop door followed by her retinue of children. Whilst she was ensconced in the office with Emma they amused themselves around the shop playing, amongst other things, I-spy, under the watchful eye of their older brother, Nathan. After about half an hour the office door opened, the women shook hands, the Jenner's entourage left and a delighted Emma shared the good news with Rosalie.

"Tessa's agreed to supply organic veggie pies and quiches and use veg each day from the Stores, along with herbs from her own market garden, to create stews and soups for the freezer. So, we'll have no waste. I've also ordered goat's milk and cheese, free range eggs and seasonal herbs and salad. We've agreed to adjust this according to demand."

"You've done well, Emma," complimented Rosalie.

"Tessa also approved my ideas for displaying the organic produce."

"That's good."

"I did decline her offer to bake cakes, for the time being. I feel I must honour Mum's arrangement with the current suppliers."

"Yes, I agree."

"Just pray that all goes well this evening when I visit Jilly."

"I will."

Any further conversation was curtailed as customers claimed their attention and they were kept busy till closing time.

It was not until the end of the day when Emma sat up in her flat eating her micro-wave dinner that the disappointment of not speaking with Roger Cooper washed over her. *He obviously had more important things to do with his time than hang around waiting for me, unless,* she pondered, *I took longer over the phone calls than I'd imagined.*

She shook herself. *It's no use sitting here, feeling morose about it, I've too much to do and I'll see him another day,* she concluded philosophically. She washed up the crockery from her meal, had a shower, changed her clothes and was in the van driving to Newton Lokesby, in record time. She was excited at the prospect of getting her cousin, Jilly, involved in the business.

CHAPTER THIRTEEN

Two days later Drew and Morag flew back to Edinburgh. The ten days they had been away from home had been crammed with activity but Drew was satisfied they had dealt with the issues, both personal and business, in as efficient a manner as possible. He was anxious that his sisters' assumption of responsibility for the Village Stores and Post Office should run smoothly because in the long term their success, he believed, would be most advantageous to him. However, he was somewhat peeved that they were stalling over the signing of the property and rental agreements he had had drawn up. He hoped it wouldn't be too long before Alex and Emma came round to his way of thinking. After all, it was only right; He was the eldest!

The bungalow now stood completely empty, forlornly bereft of the vibrancy of its former occupants. Durrant's, Uncles Roy and Gordon's building firm, had been asked to attend to some minor repairs and tackle redecoration in consultation with Alex and Graeme who, on completion, were going to move in. Emma's proposal had been whole-heartedly approved; certainly there would be more room and Alex would be on hand for the Post Office and Stores. To allow this transition to go as smoothly as possible, Aunt Bernice had offered to babysit Bethany, two days a week, and help out in the shop when necessary. Jacky Cooper also had a vacancy in the Nursery offering Bethany two morning sessions which they gratefully accepted. Graeme decided to work from home and keep an eye on his daughter one day each week thus enabling Alex to be free to run the Post Office side of operations. Opening times would be adjusted according to her availability and well-advertised locally. The girls were confident the villagers would take these arrangements on board, once they became accustomed to them, glad they still had a Post Office to go to.

Rosalie willingly agreed to increase her hours, once Emma was back at College, and Christina, too, gave half a day to work in the Village Stores. Even Stephen Cooper and Ryan Saunders called into the shop one afternoon, to lend a hand with lifting stock, and also assist Nicky with deliveries, volunteering to help out on a regular basis as and when the need arose. Alex and Emma were touched by the eagerness of so many villagers who were anxious to be part of the smooth running of the Village Stores. They thankfully accepted the willing hands that were offered.

Emma had grown to love the flat; offered to her by her parents when she reached her eighteenth birthday, to give her some independence and themselves breathing space, and elected to stay there for the time being. Its proximity to the shop was ideal; above it, yet having its own front door making it completely separate. It was where her forbears had lived when they purchased the property, to expand the original Village Stores, in 1892.

Because she was anxious to implement some of her ideas before returning to College, following the Christmas recess, Emma had taken full advantage of this nearness. With her mind focussed, her intent was to become fully acquainted with her father's working plan. So, she'd spent every spare moment digesting the files in the office and familiarising herself with the current shop layout. She had no intention of altering anything that worked well. She knew customers disliked change; she'd heard her parents speak of it when they had moved some items round. Therefore, her changes would be subtle and gradual; familiar stock on the usual shelves but introducing new lines, on the fresh and baked side, from time to time; but most of all, eye-catching window displays, allowing her artistic flare to come to the fore.

She was delighted with the outcome of her visit to Jilly Briggs. Initially, Emma had been diffident about approaching her cousin, even though Jilly was well qualified to perform the task. The reason for Jilly being out of work was not through lack of ability but because she had suffered severe depression, after losing her unborn child at five months, earlier last year. Kit Briggs, who frequently worked off-shore, disliked leaving his wife on her own for such long periods, felt Emma's offer to Jilly was an answer to prayer. By the end of the visit Jilly was fired by Emma's enthusiasm, coming up with lots of innovative ideas for pastries and ready meals and eager to see the kitchen where she was expected to work to meet this new challenge.

So absorbed had Emma become in the running of the Stores that her College assignments lay pushed to one side. This day had been a particularly hectic, yet rewarding one, in the shop, and knowing she didn't have to prepare an evening meal because she had been invited to Green Pastures, Emma decided to leave Rosalie to cope with the quiet hour to closing time and give some attention to her College work.

At his mother's insistence, Justin went to pick up Emma for the evening meal.

"She'll be shattered after being on her feet all day in the shop!"

So, at 7 o'clock that evening he stood at the door to her flat and pressed the buzzer on Emma's intercom. He waited for a few moments. Receiving no response he tried again. Up in the flat Emma was in the study engrossed in her assignment so didn't hear him. Undeterred, Justin drew his mobile phone from his pocket and tapped in Emma's number. Immediately she answered.

"Hi, Em. I'm here to escort you to Mum and Dad's."

He heard her gasp.

"Oh, Justin, time ran away with me. I'm not ready."

"Come just as you are."

"I can't!"

"'Course you can. It's only me and the oldies."

"Justin, really!!!"

He could picture her face creasing in smiles at his choice of endearment for his parents.

"I'm waiting, Em."

"But..."

"No buts, Em. Mum is serving as we speak."

"Right! I'll take you at your word and come in all my muck and glory."

The warmth of the welcome her Aunt and Uncle gave her and the genuine acceptance of her just as she was, put Emma at her ease. She felt loved, and so relaxed.

"How are you, my dear?" Roy asked kindly as they sat around the dining table enjoying the delicious meal Bernice had prepared. Tears filled Emma's eyes.

"Oh, Uncle Roy, I was fine till you asked me that," blurted out Emma. She took a moment to compose herself and then went on to explain.

"When I'm busy I seem to be coping, but it's the oddest things that suddenly bring the hurt and the tears and the dreadful sense of loss. Just walking down the backstairs the other day reminded me of Dad on Christmas Eve."

"Oh, Emma," said Aunt Bernice compassionately, reaching out and patting her arm. For a few reflective moments they each continued eating the meal before them, savouring the flavours Bernice had so subtly blended together. Roy finished the mouthful from his fork then turned again to Emma and quietly asked, "And how are you finding the business side of things?"

"Challenging," Em replied without hesitation. She finished chewing her food, looked up from her plate and began to elaborate.

"Dad was a meticulous book-keeper. He has a written record of every transaction that has taken place since he took over responsibility for the Stores."

"My word, that's some undertaking," commented Justin.

"Yes, I daren't ever hope to emulate him but I do know whom I should contact about absolutely everything to do with suppliers and tradesmen; those whose integrity he trusted and those he would never deal with again; who supplies the freshest food and who delivers promptly, also, who offers the most competitive prices."

"That really must be a help to you, dear," said Aunt Bernice.

"Mmm. It's certainly been invaluable this week as we've been re-ordering new stock to replenish the depleted shelves."

"How do you get on with Rosalie?"

"Fine. She's such an asset. She knew Dad's ways well but we're working together to develop what works best for us. I couldn't have managed without her."

"I understand Alex is keen to get the Stores computerised."

"Yes, she and Graeme have been working for some while, with Dad, devising a program suitable for the management of the shop. I don't think it will be too long before it is implemented."

"So, you'll soon be very hi-tech, then?"

"Oh, I think I shall leave most of that to Alex. She's already au fait with the Post Office system."

"Not really your forte?"

Emma shook her head.

"What about the practical side of things?"

"Some days I'm absolutely shattered; on others, such as when I'm rearranging the displays or dressing the window, I run on adrenalin late into the night."

They laughed.

"Mustn't overdo it though, dear."

"I'll try not to, Aunt Bernice," Emma assured her Aunt.

"How do you feel about the altercation with Drew?" Justin asked.

"Mystified," Emma frowned as she replied. "He seems to have changed. His whole focus appears to be on making as much money as possible from our parent's deaths." She looked directly at Roy. "He can't really make Alex and Graeme sell their home, can he? Somehow, that doesn't seem right to me."

"You don't have to worry on that score, Emma," replied Roy gently. "When Alex married Graeme your parents gave them a lump sum as a deposit on the house as they did when Drew and Morag got married. Drew didn't include his own house in the proposed sell off deal, did he?"

"No."

"Of course not; their homes are their own, not part of the business."

"Oh!"

"Did you know your Mum and Dad also set up an account for you with a similar amount for the day when you should get married and look to buy your own home?"

Emma looked at him astonished and said quietly, "I didn't know that."

"I've seen the pass book so I know it exists. I'm surprised Alex or Drew haven't mentioned it; one of them must have come across it as they sorted out the bungalow, probably in the safe."

"Nothing's been said, but why would they be secretive about it?"

It was Roy's turn to shake his head.

"Like you, I've been somewhat perturbed by Drew's attitude so, I've had a quiet word with my solicitor, who also acted for your father. He's made a few discreet enquiries in the right quarter. As a result, the bank has frozen your parent's personal assets, pending probate, but the business account remains active now that you and Alex are signatories."

"What about reimbursing Drew for a third of the value of the stock and paying him a percentage of the shop takings each month? Where do we stand over that rental agreement he thrust at us?"

"What?" Justin looked at Emma aghast. "You are joking, Em!" he exploded.

"No, I'm not. Drew is adamant that is what he is legally entitled to."

"Nonsense! That simply can't be right. He's taken it too far. Hasn't he, Dad?" Justin appealed to Roy.

Before replying, Roy pushed his empty plate further onto the table, leaned his elbows on the hard surface, linked his fingers under his chin and contemplated his words carefully.

"I do find it all rather high-handed so..." Roy began but Justin butted in as his father was speaking. "How can he have had legal documents drawn up so quickly? It's Christmas and New Year and surely..."

"Yes, son, I'd already considered that. I, too, was of the opinion that legal offices were closed over the holiday period so, drawing on my acquaintance with Adam Catton I was able to gain the ear of his boss, Jocelyn Capps-Walker, my own solicitor, at his home. He has kindly agreed to go through everything with a fine tooth comb and act on your behalf should that become necessary."

Emma looked up in horror, "Surely it won't come to that?"

"I hope not but Drew does appear to have overstepped the mark somewhat, in our view, and he also seems so sure about his legal rights that I felt it only right that you and Alex should have unbiased legal representation, too."

"Perhaps Scottish law differs to English law in these matters," suggested Bernice as she rose to clear away the plates.

"Even so, the girls need to know where they stand. I noted too, that the dental practice Drew and Morag own in Edinburgh was not included in his proposed sell off deal, yet I know for a fact that your parents financed the setting up of the practice when Drew concluded his training." Both Emma and Justin gasped in surprise. Uncle Roy smiled at them both. "News to you?" They nodded. "Well, we'll leave it for now and let the legal minds sort it out," Roy commented firmly.

"Yes. Thankyou, Uncle Roy, for all you've done for us."

The remainder of the mealtime passed by pleasantly enough and after helping with the dishes Justin and Emma gravitated towards the sun-lounge.

"A bit different to when we last met in here," said Justin.

"Yes," replied Emma thoughtfully "such a lot seems to have happened in just a short space of time."

Justin nodded then cautiously enquired, "Dare I ask how you are coping with personal issues, without you biting my head off?"

Emma's head shot round quickly to face Justin, "Oh, Justin, I was awful, wasn't I? I don't know how everyone put up with my appalling temperamental behaviour. My one regret is being unable to apologise to Mum and Dad for all the angst I caused them."

"My dear Em, they witnessed the work of grace in your life," Justin fervently assured her.

"But it's only since they've been gone that I've learned what trust really means."

"They saw the change in you and were wise enough to know that growing in the grace and knowledge of our Lord Jesus takes a life-time."

"Mm, I suppose you're right. I feel I still have so much to learn, though," she said ruefully.

"As do we all," Justin murmured in agreement.

"Coffee's ready," Bernice's voice called through the doorway so they made their way to the sitting room. When the cups were in their hands, Justin spoke softly, "Em, you didn't really answer my question about personal issues; Roger, for instance?"

Emma walked unhurriedly over to the window and peered at the harbour lights through the darkness. This action gave her time to think before replying.

"Roger?" Emma looked up at him bemused.

"Yes, Roger; that dishy doctor who's had eyes only for you since he arrived home on Christmas Eve," said Justin with a chuckle.

"Do you honestly think I would discuss with you my feelings for Roger when I haven't spoken with him about them?" she tossed her head in typical Emma fashion.

"You do have feelings, then?" her cousin gently probed.

"Justin, you're impossible!" replied Emma emphatically, quickly averting her flaming cheeks.

"My dear Emma, you don't have to answer, your face says it all."

Shaking her head she turned back to face him, "You!" she mouthed playfully, then concentrated on drinking her coffee.

"Em, come and sit down. I need to tell you something."

"Tease, more like," she grinned at him but complied with his wishes and sat down at one end of the sofa.

Sitting, either side of the blazing hearth, Bernice and Roy exchanged a knowing look. They were each aware what the other was thinking as they watched and listened to Emma. The difference in her behaviour and attitude was a delight to behold and they gave thanks to God for the change they could see in their niece. While the young folk chatted the older couple sat in quiet contemplation, the warmth from the burning logs lulling them into a sleepy haze.

Justin finished his coffee, placed his cup on the side table, and then sat back, carefully crossing his legs so he was in a position to look directly at his cousin.

"Em, I won't beat about the bush. I need to speak with you about Roger. He came to see me before he returned to his hospital."

Emma lifted up her head. "He's gone back?"

"Yes, didn't you know?"

She lowered her eyes and slowly shook her head a heavy, sinking feeling settling around her heart.

"He didn't say goodbye," she murmured, suddenly regretting the busyness of the last few days.

"What I have to say may have some bearing on that."

"Oh?" intrigued she raised her eyes and glanced expectantly at Justin.

"You may not at this time wish to discuss feelings you may have, but Roger's position towards you has obviously altered. In the absence of your father he approached Drew to acquaint him with this fact, and in old fashioned parlance, seek permission to court you."

Emma cocked her head and raised her eyebrows and with wide open eyes stared at him in incredulous surprise, "Really?"

"Yes; I think Roger felt he was doing the honourable thing by speaking with Drew first but apparently Drew gave him short shrift."

"Whatever do you mean?" she asked sharply.

"Drew told him in no uncertain manner to keep away from you."

"What?" the colour drained from her face and her shoulders sagged as she sat limply in her seat.

Alarmed by her reaction to his words Justin was uncertain how to proceed. He paused for a few moments and took time to pray silently for wisdom to deal with the situation as kindly and fairly as he could. Feeling Emma would prefer openness he continued to relay his conversation with Roger to her.

"Drew's statement to Roger went along the lines that you did not need a poor, penny-pinching trainee doctor come fortune hunting. When you were a penniless student you were the butt of his caustic wit and sarcasm now that you're an heiress he needn't turn on the charm in the hopes of winning you."

"Oh, dear," tears filled her eyes as she put her head in her hands. She was stunned.

Justin moved along the sofa and put his arm across her shoulders. "I'm so very sorry, Em."

After a few moments Emma spoke quietly, "He's changed, you know, so changed."

Justin had to bite his tongue to stop himself from blurting out, "Who?" It was very evident that both men were behaving differently. He needed to be patient. Given time Emma would intimate whom she was thinking about.

"So changed!" she murmured with a shake of the head.

They sat for some moments in contemplatative silence, each absorbed in their own thoughts, and then Justin quietly went on to explain.

"Following the cool reception from Drew, Roger called round here. He was quite perplexed about the whole situation but also anxious not to cause difficulties between you and your brother. He so wanted the opportunity to speak with you, Emma, but every time he tried to get near you someone from the family was hovering protectively by or else you were unavailable because you were busy with shop business."

Emma, silent and pale-faced, listened intently. Slowly she shook her head, deep regrets again washing over her for being so engrossed in work at the Stores during the last few days. She recalled the day Roger peeped around the office door and that when later she had looked for him, after making her phone calls, he had gone. She had searched all the aisles but he was nowhere to be seen.

An occasion after Church flashed into her mind. She had been standing with Drew and Morag when Roger had approached them. Drew had instantly grabbed her elbow and steered her towards the door to speak with the Vicar. Emma had thought nothing about his conduct at the time, had smiled at Roger as their eyes met as she walked past him, thinking that Drew wanted to converse with Hugh whilst he was free. She had not attributed ulterior motives to his actions.

All at once Emma realised that, in subsequent days, she had been so preoccupied with her projects for the shop, people and other issues had faded into the recess of her mind. With shock she grasped the import of the discovery that her busyness had been to obliterate the hurt caused by her parents' accident not aimed to deliberately to keep friends at arm's length. She missed her parents more than she could say. She missed Dad's sense of humour and even her Mum's no-nonsense approach to life. Mum was always straight and down to earth but Dad's merry laughter could squeeze a joke out of a stone.

However, Roger was a friend, a real friend. He'd proved that in the early difficult days following the accident. He had listened and he had shown her genuine care. Was he more than a friend? Emma's heart seemed to somersault over at this thought. Did she want him to be more than a friend, having kept him at arm's length for so many years? She certainly felt more relaxed in his presence than she ever had before.

Justin waited patiently as he watched differing emotions flicker across Emma's face.

"So, that's why he didn't say goodbye."

"Yes," said Justin, "but he left you this."

Justin pulled an envelope out from his pocket and handed it to her. He then sat back, closed his eyes in order to give Emma privacy in which to read the words Roger had penned to her, and also to pray for her.

"My dear Emma, I wish with all my heart I was saying these words to you, face to face. As you are now reading this, you will know the reason it is not so. It was good to see you again, Emma, and speak, if only briefly, of the changes in our lives. I would welcome the opportunity of continuing our discussion about the differences our new understanding of the power and presence of the Lord Jesus has made. I liked what I saw of the new Emma and would relish getting to know her better but I was denied…"

The words swam before Emma's eyes as they filled with tears and it was some time before she was able to continue reading.

"I appreciate our time together was very short and so many things were left unsaid…"

In her mind's eye she saw Roger standing in the porch of his parent's home on Christmas Eve, so tall and handsome, and remembered the kindly way he had spoken to her, no hint of malice or sarcasm. She could not forget how supportive he had been when she and Alex had received the news of their parent's death. Dad would have approved of his caring demeanour. Even when she'd been so rude and brushed him aside Roger had stayed there, right beside her, solid, dependable. On Boxing Day the manner in which they had opened up to one another, after a tentative start, about the heart changing experiences that were so new and challenging to them both, had been a comfortable time of sharing.

Momentarily, a dreamy smile lit Emma's face. She, too, liked the "new" Roger. Why ever did Drew disapprove of them getting better acquainted?

Justin caught the change in her countenance as a puzzled frown furrowed Emma's brow. He leant forward.

"Are you alright, Em?"

Emma had been lost in her thoughts and fleetingly forgotten Justin's presence.

She looked across at him and nodded.

"Why doesn't Drew want Roger to have contact with me?"

"I can't answer that, Em, because I don't know. You'd have to ask Drew."

"That won't be easy to do because he's a bit unapproachable at the moment."

Emma got up from the sofa abruptly, stood facing Justin with hands on her hips, a fiery spark in her eyes, and said indignantly, "You know, he has no right to dictate who does or does not see me. This is the twenty-first century not the Victorian era!"

"Oh, Em," said Justin with an exasperated sigh.

"It's OK, Justin," Emma assured him with a smile and relaxed her arms down by her side.

"I'm not spoiling for a fight. I'm more sad than angry that Drew didn't feel able to discuss the situation with me. To put the record straight, I was never a penniless student, Dad saw to that, and neither am I, as far as I am aware, an heiress to an earthly inheritance, although I am rich beyond measure with the abundant blessings the Lord daily showers on me."

"We are very blessed," Justin agreed, thinking of the blessing the witness of his cousin now was.

"I am constantly amazed at God's patience with me when I continually let Him down."

"His grace is immeasurable, Em, and thankfully covers all situations."

Emma looked at him dubiously.

"Even the aggro with Drew and the uncertainty with Roger?"

Justin looked at Emma with compassion, and then smiled as he slowly nodded his head.

"Even affairs of the heart."

Emma sat bolt upright. "I'll write to them both," she said decisively. "I was going to leave it hoping the passage of time would make the situation easier, but I feel I must deal with it now, so I'll write. Please pray for me, that I'll be able to express my feelings clearly and that they won't misunderstand or, as far as Drew is concerned, take umbrage."

Justin leaned over and touched her arm affectionately.

"You know I'll always willingly give you my prayerful support, Em. You can depend on that. Just remember not to dictate to God His own agenda."

With a smile on her lips she gratefully murmured, "Thanks, Justin."

"Why not have a chat with Alex. Maybe she can help to iron out one or two things."

"Good idea! I might do that," Emma replied thoughtfully.

Chapter Fourteen

Some weeks later, Emma was huddled in the Norwich bus station, a howling wind swirling around the shelter she was standing beneath. She was longing to be at home in the warmth of her flat and looked hopefully, through the murky glass, for the bus. There weren't many people about, and as she was an hour earlier than usual even the noisy school children were absent from the waiting queue.

"Hello, Emma," a voice called, "too bad the buses can't keep to timetables," it complained.

"We wouldn't be standin' 'ere gettin' wet and cold if they was on schedule," joined in someone else grumpily.

She turned to see Mrs Saunders and another lady from the village laden with shopping bags. Emma smiled and exchanged greetings with them but the women's continual moaning irked her somewhat.

"There's always a valid reason for delays, usually something beyond the driver's control," she explained pleasantly but her fellow passengers persisted with their complaints.

Grumbling is an infectious social disease that robs us, and all those around us, of joy, she thought, *I'm not going to be drawn into their annoyance.*

However, it was difficult to shut out their loud-mouthed conversation.

"'ave yew 'eard, they've took on that Cook girl in the shop?"

"Noo!" was the disbelieving reply.

"Fancy, working alongside the daughter of the man who killed yow'n parents!"

"The papers say the verdict will be out later this week."

"'bout time!"

"'Ope it's a bit stiffer than that they give bor Josh."

Deliberately, Emma turned to look again through the dirty window pane, hoping the bus would miraculously put in an appearance, and then stamped her feet in an effort to keep warm. She had spent a busy, yet rewarding, few days at college and her mind lingered over recent activities she had been involved in. How she had enjoyed the infectious delight of the class she was currently working with. Their insatiable appetite for knowledge certainly kept her on her toes.

She spoke quietly from her heart to her Heavenly Father. This had become a conscious habit, since her conversation with Justin, particularly when she wanted to avoid negative thoughts or obliterate activity or chatter that she didn't find wholesome or want to be a part of. *I have much to be thankful for, Father. The day's gone well but I am looking forward to being home,* she started but then the overheard gossip impinged on her thoughts.

Dear, Father God, help me to accept whatever the court decides about Joe and Josh Cook's involvement in Mum and Dad's accident. Thankyou for the peace You have given to me on this issue. I am now convinced they are with You in heaven. Nothing a jury decides can bring them back. I think, too, we did the right thing by offering the Saturday job to Maxine Cook. She wasn't responsible for her father's, or brother's, actions and she's proving to be quite adept at shop work. Thankyou, too, for my caring and supportive family, I'm sure I'll have a lovely time with Alex and Graeme and dear little Bethany this evening, and hopefully there'll be a letter waiting for me from Roger.

Her heart somersaulted over at this prospect. Since the day she had replied to the note Roger had left with her cousin,

Justin, they had corresponded, fairly frequently, and spoken on the phone a couple of times a week, and managed to meet up on his days' off-duty. Roger's attentive, yet positive approach had done much to uplift her spirit, particularly after the curt missive she had received from her brother, Drew, warning her not to do anything foolish. However, she and Roger had agreed they wanted to get to know one another better. Although the miles separated them, they were willing to use the means that were, at the present time, most available to them to keep in touch, and explore that possibility.

Quite spontaneously her thoughts shifted to the regular pattern that had developed over the last few weeks; Tuesday, Wednesday and Thursday were College days, Friday and Saturday were shop days. Mondays were split; with mornings devoted to office work and attending to shop orders, as well as dealing with suppliers, while the afternoons were spent in preparation for teaching practice on Tuesday at one of the City schools.

As Aunt Bernice did not have Bethany or work in the Stores on Monday she insisted on preparing an evening meal for Emma. This arrangement also enabled Emma to join the House Group held at Green Pastures on that evening and enjoy Bible Study and fellowship. She was pleased about this because the group were considering what the Bible had to say about the Christian's attitude. In the past this had been a contentious issue for Emma in her dealings with her parents and Roger and, if she were honest, most people. It was proving an instructive and enlightening exercise.

On Tuesdays, Emma caught the early morning bus, outside the Stores, in company with the school children and College students travelling into the city. She spent the two nights in Norwich with Graeme's parents, who lived within walking distance of the university building where she met with her tutors.

Today was Thursday and when she returned home on Thursdays she generally did her washing and other household chores. When these were complete she made her way to her sister's house to share a meal, and afterwards babysit Bethany, so that Alex and Graeme could attend the young marrieds' house fellowship, held at Adam and Laura's home.

If her tutors were really benevolent, and finished tutorials earlier than scheduled, she was able to get home in time to go for a walk along the beach. Emma found this invigorating; paradoxically it cleared her mind but also enabled her to think.

Sunday was Church day and she would allow nothing to interfere with her attendance at the morning and evening service. Worship had become precious to her. Sometimes, different friends or family members invited her for Sunday lunch, which she happily accepted. However, she was not averse to spending time alone and on such occasions Emma took opportunity to read a book or write letters. Alternatively, on a fine day she enjoyed a walk down to the quay or the shore with a sketch pad and pencil in her hand.

This is what she had planned to do on her return home today but the weather had turned, at lunch time, from cold and sunny to blustery rain.

Not conducive to pleasant strolls and sketching, she thought to herself just as the bus drew up at the stop. As she climbed aboard a blast of warm air hit her and she sat down thankful that the vehicle's heating system was working efficiently.

At the bus stop near the hospital a wet, bedraggled passenger boarded the bus. Emma gave her only a cursory glance, then as she stumbled along the bus, recognised it was her friend, Jansy.

"Hi, Jans," Emma called, "come and sit here."

Jansy plonked herself on the offered seat so grateful to rest her aching legs.

"It's good to see you, Jans," said Emma affectionately, "it seems such a long time since we got together. How are you? How are the plans going for your wedding? Have you finally decided on the colours for your flowers and the bridesmaid's dresses?" she asked, giving her friend time to catch her breath and push back the hood of her anorak.

"I'm so glad to sit down," Jansy gasped. "It's been a rather hectic day."

"Are you going home? Is it your day off tomorrow?"

Jansy nodded.

"How's Dave? Is he home or at sea?"

"At sea, due home on Saturday."

"Have you found somewhere to live when you're married? Did the cottage appeal to you?"

"Dave liked it but we haven't reached a final decision. I would still favour living in the city but Dave isn't too keen so...." The two friends continued to catch up with each other's news as the bus proceeded on its journey towards Newton Westerby. They were unaware of the falling darkness or the wintry elements surrounding them, so absorbed were they in their conversation.

Emma was keen to know the details of Jansy's wedding plans and her aspirations for the future but Jansy quickly changed the subject.

"What have you heard about Josh and his Dad?"

"Josh's trial finished on Tuesday."

"Were you called as a witness?"

"No, but Alex thought she might have to give evidence in connexion with one of the charges against him.

"Whatever for?"

"She served him when he withdrew money fraudulently from the Post Office. However, it wasn't necessary because Josh pleaded guilty."

"How is that related to your Mum and Dad's accident?"

"It's not; it's to do with him stealing Mrs Jenner's pension card and drawing all the money out."

Jansy frowned, "But what about the charge against Joe and Josh for causing the car accident?"

"That isn't being dealt with at the moment. The police are still building their case against the perpetrators of the crash."

"Well, I think they ought to get a move on. Surely the most serious crime should be dealt with first. You don't want this hanging over your head indefinitely."

"The wheels of the justice system must be allowed to move in their time honoured way."

"Emma!" Jansy looked at her friend in disbelief. "What has come over you? It's not like you to be so tolerant."

Emma gravely shook her head. "I'm gradually learning patience, Jans. Anyway, the outcome of the case against Josh resulted in him being sentenced to spend time in a Young Offender's Institute."

"And how long is he likely to be there?"

"Eighteen months for the attack on Nicky."

Jansy gasped. "That's not long for what he did!"

"Well, no one was allowed into the Youth Court, apart from Michelle, but apparently he pleaded not guilty to attempting to murder Nicky though he did admit to grievous bodily harm. Sentences for all his other offences will run concurrently."

"What nonsense!"

"The fact that it is a first time offence was taken into consideration so…"

"But that's ridiculous," Jansy raised her voice indignantly, "how does the punishment fit the crime? Shakespeare said "the law is an ass" and a sentence like that would suggest he is right. And we all know it's not the first crime Josh has committed; just the first time he's been caught!"

"Calm down, Jans, I only hope Josh gets some help to turn his life around while he is inside."

"Oh yes, I can just see a bunch of do-gooders lining up to reform Josh," she muttered sarcastically.

"The verdict on Joe is expected tomorrow."

"I assume it won't be as lenient as Josh's."

"We'll have to wait and see."

⚛⚛

Later, when her hands were busy with suds in the sink, as she washed a couple of jumpers, Emma reflected on the conversation with Jansy. She was perturbed at the consternation the remembrance of it caused her. As she continued to mull this thought over in her mind Emma was shocked to realise that Jansy's position, at the hospital, seemed to be more important to her than her future role as Dave's wife. Most of her friend's plans revolved, in the main, around her own desires and ambitions, and not a shared anticipation of building a life and home together with her fiancé. This attitude really puzzled Emma, particularly when only a few months earlier Jansy had been so excited at the prospect of becoming Mrs Dave Ransome.

I would go to the ends of the earth to be with Roger, even if it meant living in a mud hut, Emma thought to herself, dreamily. She then jumped back from the sink as she turned the tap on too full and the water splashed all over her front.

Concentrate, Girl, as Dad would say, she scolded herself. *You hardly know the man!* She shook her head vigorously. Her embryonic relationship with the changed Roger was so very new; nonetheless, the peace within her heart at this moment seemed to confirm the rightness of it.

Thankyou, Lord for giving me this calm assurance; Alex was correct, she said I would just know if it was right or not and a sure indication that I cared would be when my heart and mind were in unison about my feelings for Roger. I think that's the stage I've reached at the moment. I'm certainly not plagued with doubts and uncertainty anymore, but I do wish Dad were here to talk things through.

"Emma, would you like to celebrate your graduation at the Maid's Head Restaurant or would you prefer a family gathering at Aunt Bernice's?" Alex asked some weeks later as the sisters worked together in the kitchen following the usual Thursday evening meal they shared together. "The choice is all yours," she added with a smile.

"Oh, Alex," Emma started then swallowed hard because a lump had caught in her throat, "that was always our "special place" to mark a particular occasion with Mum and Dad, wasn't it? I really don't want to put anyone to too much trouble."

"It's no trouble at all. We would just like to acknowledge your achievement in a way that will be special for you."

"Having you and Graeme there at the ceremony, along with Roger, will be special for me."

"And afterwards?" Alex pressed her sister.

"A family gathering with Aunt Bernice and Uncle Roy will be just fine."

"Aunt Bernice will be delighted with that response. I'll let her know to go ahead with the plans."

Emma chuckled, "You had it all arranged, didn't you?"

"Well, we had a fair idea what your choice would be."

The day of Emma's graduation finally arrived and was greeted by an early morning sun rising from a horizon where blue sky and azure sea meet. She had woken early and chosen to walk down to the beach and stroll along the water's edge, her heart so full of many different emotions; thankfulness that she had achieved the academic success, of which many, said she was not capable; sadness that Mum and Dad were not there to participate in the euphoria of the day; disappointment, too, that her life-long friend, Jansy, would not be sharing the occasion with her; excitement that Roger had managed to negotiate time off to attend; contentment that she would be surrounded by family and friends who had lovingly and prayerfully supported her during the last few months; gratitude, also, for the selfless giving of the hard-working staff at the Village Stores; joy at the continuing graciousness of God to her.

Emma stood on the sand, and gazed out at the gently rolling waves, overwhelmed by the intensity of feeling that welled up inside her. Watching the ceaseless repetition of the ripples lapping at her feet brought into her mind verses from Lamentations, Uncle Roy had quoted at the last house-group fellowship, concerning the love and compassion of God that never fails, but is new every morning.

Dear, Father God, thankyou for Your love that comes to me fresh each new day; forgiving me, holding me, caring for me.

How great is Your faithfulness. I just want to thank and praise You for it.

For some moments Emma remained in quiet contemplation, marvelling at the splendour of the sea in front of her, and felt the presence of the Creator God completely surround her. The breaking waves tossed a prettily marked shell at her feet. She bent down to pick it up. As she cradled the fragile structure in her palm she carefully turned it over with the fore-finger of her right hand. She was disappointed to find that it was broken, yet its imperfection did not detract from the beauty of the markings and colours. At that moment, it seemed to Emma, the little shell was symbolic of the delicate balance of life. It had become spoiled by the relentless pounding of the waves yet it still retained its attractiveness.

Not many months ago her heart had been broken by the cruel circumstances of life but God hadn't tossed her aside, even though Emma had blamed Him for the terrible buffeting she had received. In her brokenness and despair the Lord had come to her through the kindly hands of Aunt Bernice, the wise counsel of Uncle Roy and the straight talking of cousin Justin, as well as the faithful ministry of praying friends. She was amazed that despite her imperfections God loved her, and although He hadn't removed her temper He had taught her, by His grace, how to deal with it. Looking back over the past few months it seemed incredible to her that, in her sinful state, He'd seen a glimmer of the loveliness she could become and offered her His salvation.

A seagull squawked overhead and the sudden noise made Emma jump and disturbed the reflective atmosphere that enveloped her. She turned from the shoreline, her fingers wrapped around the tiny shell that had provoked such pensive thoughts, and made her way home across the beach. Her feet quickened as she reached the lane and her heart beat faster with excitement as she anticipated all that lay before her in this day.

"What a perfectly splendid meal, Mrs Durrant," complimented Roger warmly.

"Yes, Aunt Bernice, thank you for choosing all my favourite food. It was delicious," echoed Emma.

"It has been my pleasure and no less than you deserve, my dear," said Bernice rising from the table in order to clear the dirty crockery. "I'll just see to these pots and then serve coffee in about an hour, if that's alright with everyone."

Trixie and Alex got up simultaneously and together said, "I'll give a hand." They laughed and proceeded to the kitchen laden with glasses and plates to find Justin had already made a start on the washing up. He looked up as they opened the door.

"Oh, good, reinforcements! I'm running out of space on the draining board. Someone grab a tea towel."

With much hilarity and numerous willing hands the tedious task was soon accomplished and Graeme offered to make the coffee, with assistance from Justin, when everyone was ready.

In the meantime the others left the dining room and wandered through into the spacious sitting room where the afternoon sun was dancing on the crystal ornaments Bernice had displayed on the deep window sills. The morning's ceremony was still the main topic of conversation.

"I thought you looked lovely in your gown, Emma, so regal. My heart swelled with pride as you climbed the steps to the podium. What an achievement! Well done, my girl," congratulated Roy.

Emma turned to her uncle in surprise, knowing that she had been allocated only three tickets for specially invited guests and these had been given to Alex, Graeme and Roger.

"How ever did you see me?" she asked.

Roy's eyes twinkled as he replied, "What's the point of having contacts in strategic places if you don't make use of them? For once, I pulled the right strings, at the right time. I wasn't going to miss my dearest girl's special day, not for anything!" He came up to Emma, put his arm affectionately around her shoulders and kissed her cheek. "You've done so very well, Emma."

"Yes, a tremendous attainment, Emma," agreed Doctor John with feeling as he patted her on the back.

"I'm sure I don't deserve all these accolades," she replied diffidently, slowly shaking her head.

"Why not?"

Smiling, Roger came towards her, took hold of her hand and drew her to sit beside him on the sofa.

"Of course you do," he said gently. "You've worked very hard and that hard work has now been recognised."

"We're all so pleased at your success, Emma. Here you are, my dear, have a coffee," said Bernice as she distributed steaming cups from the tray that Graeme was holding. "Your Mum and Dad would have been so proud. If only they had lived they would have celebrated this day in style. You know they would. So, we've done it for them."

"Oh, Aunt Bernice," said Emma, tears coursing down her cheeks unbidden.

Roger reached out and tenderly touched her face to stem the flow of salty tear-drops. At the same time he pulled a handkerchief out of his pocket and handed it to her.

"She's right, you know." Roger paused, and then chose his words with care as Emma dabbed at her eyes. "Don't you think they would have approved marking your success with a family party? Hosting a special occasion is what your Mum did best and your Aunt and Uncle have upheld family honour with their excellent hospitality."

She peeked at him through the hanky, nodded then, gave him a teary smile.

"Hear, hear," echoed Alex and Graeme.

Doctor John also nodded his assent and then declared in his good natured way, "This has been a wonderful day, Emma, and we're honoured to have been invited to celebrate it with you in such a fine manner."

Emma took a deep breath then smiled at him through her tears.

"Thankyou for your kindness," she replied, knowing that the Doctor was giving her the opportunity to regain her composure. With Roger's assistance she got to her feet. Rising to her full stature she looked around the room at them all and assuming the air of confidence they had come to expect from her in recent weeks she addressed these people who were so dear to her.

"I would like to convey my sincerest thanks to you all for coming today; for the delicious meal and entertaining company and for the beautiful flowers and delightful gifts and cards that mysteriously appeared overnight up in my flat."

There was muffled laughter in the room.

Emma's eyes lit up, "I don't think I need ask who was responsible for that little escapade, do I, Justin?" She swung round and looked directly at her cousin.

"Me, Em?" Justin asked innocently.

"Yes, Justin, you!" Emma teased light-heartedly. Everyone joined in the merriment, glad that the sombre mood had lifted, anxious to ensure the memory of her graduation day was a happy one for Emma.

"How do you feel about finally attaining your goal, Emma?" Trixie asked.

"Amazed and grateful," Emma replied with a smile. "I still remember the parent-teacher meeting, about twelve years ago, when Miss Pedwardine told Mum and Dad not to be too disappointed that I was not academic material but that I would probably do well as a shop assistant. I was devastated. Last week she came into the Stores specifically to apologise for saying those things. She went on to say that, as the third child, it's difficult to live under the shadow of clever elder siblings; Drew apparently sauntered through his academic accomplishments, whereas Alex plodded towards her achievements, apart from Maths, for which she had a particular gifted aptitude, and then there was me. "But, you, Emma, were so wilful; it was hard to see you ever being proficient at anything," she reminded me and then came right up to me, took hold of my arm and said, "You've proved us all wrong. Well done!. Your father would have been so proud of you, young lady, don't throw it away." She then proceeded to congratulate me on my honours degree and wish me well in the future, but her parting words were, "Don't waste your achievements in a shop." It seems I can't win! I was pleased to be able to tell her that I had been offered and accepted two days teaching at the village school. I truly appreciate Rosalie, and the team we have at the Stores, for making it feasible for me to accept this part-time post. I really had resigned myself to foregoing that possibility to concentrate on running the shop."

"Thankyou for sharing that experience with us, Emma. We all pray everything will work out well for you. Just don't try to do too much."

"Oh, that's not likely. I have much to thank Mum for, not least, her organizational skills. She taught us to use our time wisely, allocate each task a slot and stick to it. I still do that." A number of heads in the room nodded in assent, knowing how true that was.

CHAPTER FIFTEEN

Within a short space of time the sunshine and the splendid floral display drew Emma and Roger out through the French windows. It wasn't too long before the rest of the family spilled over into the garden to join them. Both Bernice and Roy loved to potter amongst the plants; she enjoyed experimenting with the vast pallet of annual colour, the different seasons offered, and he liked the challenge afforded by the defined lines of the lawns, the clipped yew and privet and the structural elegance of the shrubs and trees. They also enjoyed sharing their garden with those who appreciated the ambience they strove to create.

As they strolled, Emma's senses reeled with the heady scent of the early roses, as well as an awareness of the nearness of Roger's presence.

It wasn't too long before Roger took hold of Emma's hand. She glanced up at him but didn't pull it away. It fitted; it felt right; it made her heart beat faster, yet she also felt happy and secure. For a few more minutes they wandered leisurely along the gravel path, in company with other family members, but, as different ones stopped to admire a plant or sample the fragrance of certain flowers, Emma and Roger soon found themselves ambling on the footpath alone. It traversed the orchard, skirted Roy's tomato greenhouse, and ended at the far side of the vegetable patch in front of a gate in the boundary hedge.

Neither of them could have described in detail what they passed by, so absorbed were they in one another's company. Imperceptibly, Roger opened the latch on the gate. They walked through and followed the well-trodden track across the rough land that meandered down to the bank at the river's edge. Talking stopped as they stood side by side to watch the swift flowing water carry some flotsam further upstream.

After a short time, Roger stepped in front of Emma, took up both her hands and held them together on his chest in his own finely structured surgeon's hands. He bent his head to tenderly kiss the tips of her fingers.

"Dearest Em, this has truly been a momentous day."

Emma lifted her head to meet his gaze. "Yes," she agreed, "thanks to you and the family."

He smiled.

"I rather like this new, gracious Emma Kemp more than I can say. She doesn't bite my head off or stamp on my toes."

Emma laughed, and then replied in similar vein.

"And I like this new, kind, considerate Roger Cooper who doesn't fight me, tooth and nail, every time we meet."

Still clasping her hands to his chest with one hand, Roger gently drew her head on to his shoulder with his free hand, and whispered into her ear, "I feel I could readily spend the rest of my life with this certain changed person."

Emma made to pull away from him but Roger held her firmly.

"Really?" was all she managed to say.

"Yes, really," he confirmed.

Thus enfolded, they continued to stand together, savouring the moment. Time seemed to pause, temporarily. The stillness was only broken by the rippling water and the calling seabirds. Then, for a second, Roger relaxed his hold. Emma took advantage of this, drew back, tossed her auburn head, Emma-like, and with hands on her hips and feet apart looked at him askance and then demanded with a sparkle in her eyes, "Roger Cooper, was that a proposal of marriage or did my ears deceive me?"

Roger slowly folded his arms and stood gazing at her, nonchalantly.

"Oh, your hearing was spot on."

"You tease!"

Their eyes locked in a moment of tenderness.

Roger flung his arms open wide and Emma moved quickly into the shelter of their embrace.

"Emma Louisa Kemp, I love you. Will you marry me?"

"I love you, too, Roger," Emma sighed contentedly and relaxed in his arms.

Roger ran his fingers through the soft, silken tresses of her hair as he bent to kiss her brow.

"My beautiful Carrots!"

"You haven't called me that since last Christmas Eve."

"I didn't dare. I really didn't want to upset you."

"I was impossible, wasn't I?"

Roger smiled ruefully.

"At times, things were somewhat fraught!"

Emma looked up into his handsome, caring face.

"Not anymore," she vowed.

"Grace and love have worked such miracles in our lives, haven't they?"

"Yes," she agreed "I thank God, each day, for His infinite patience with us."

"It's going to be a life-long learning process, Em," said Roger as he slowly drew his finger down the side of her face in a gentle caress, "but there's no one I'd rather share it with than you." Then, he tilted her chin and lightly brushed his lips against her upturned mouth.

"You haven't answered my question, Miss Kemp, so I don't know if I should really be doing this," said Roger quietly.

"Well, what do you think?"

"I need you to tell me."

"You do?"

"Oh yes!"

"Can you live with my hair?"

If he was surprised at the question Roger gave no indication but simply replied, "I think your hair is the most gorgeous colour imaginable. I have always admired the richness of it. I know you have to wear it up when you're working in the shop but I prefer it most when it's hanging freely down your back."

"I constantly thought you hated it."

"Why do you think I used to try and find all those adjectives to describe it?"

"To taunt me."

"Oh, Em."

"Alex suggested you were being complimentary but I didn't believe her."

"Oh, my dear precious, Carrots.

Roger hugged her tenderly and buried his face in her red hair, then cupped her face delicately in his hands.

"I just love the feel, the smell and the colour of your hair. I love the way it frames your face. I love the way it dances when you toss your head. I love the way it bounces when you walk. Shall I go on?"

"No. I never knew."

"Carrots has been my pet name for you, forever. Not in a derogatory manner but always with the greatest of affection. I'm sorry you didn't realise. I certainly didn't intend to cause you hurt. I hope I shall be more sensitive to your feelings in the future."

"Yes!" she said decisively.

"Yes?" he queried.

"Yes, I will marry you."

"Because I like your hair?"

"No, because I love you. I like your openness and honesty and I think we will learn to speak frankly with one another about everything so there won't be any more misunderstandings."

Roger beamed at her, his eyes reflecting the radiant love emanating from her face.

"You were always outspoken and forthright, Em. I think that's why sparks flew so ferociously between us particularly when we were teenagers."

"It's good to clear the air with straight talking, but from now on our moments of intense discussion will be tempered with love rather than ignited by temper."

"I'm rather glad about that because I have no wish to be constantly falling out with you. This is a sign of my intent and a token of my pledge to you."

Roger clasped her left hand, drew it through the crook of his arm, and carefully laid her fingers along his forearm. He reached into his jacket pocket and pulled out a deep crimson, velvet box, which he placed into Emma's right hand, lifting the lid as he did so.

Emma gasped and her eyes opened wide as she viewed the contents.

"Sapphires," she whispered.

"To match the colour of your eyes," he said transferring the circlet of blue stones from its nestling place in the box to a position of prominence on Emma's ring finger.

Still holding her hand Roger vowed, "I love you now, my dearest Emma and I will love you for always," then he lovingly embraced her and sealed his declaration with a tender kiss.

They pulled apart their eyes still locked.

"You are very desirable, my luscious Carrots, but that loveliness is not mine to share until our wedding day," Roger spoke softly yet sensitively.

Even so, Emma's face glowed as crimson as the ring box in her hand and she rapidly shook her hair forwards.

"My precious Carrots, you'll never be able to keep any secrets from me. Come on, let's go and share our good news."

Roger made to grab her hand but Emma deftly evaded his action.

He looked at her quizzically.

Quietly she said, "Can we keep this to ourselves? It is something so special; I just want to savour the joy of you and the overwhelming happiness our love has brought."

"You'll have a job to hide it. Your face is such a giveaway. It radiates." Emma smiled as he spoke.

"Just the family, then; no big announcement," she appealed earnestly.

"What are you afraid of, Em?"

"Nothing! I'm just mindful that Jansy and Dave were equally as euphoric when they became engaged and I still don't understand what went wrong between them."

"Emma, we must leave our friends in the Lord's hands."

Emma shook herself. "Yes, you're right. I am being rather faithless in this matter."

"We'll work to encourage one another in the faith as the Bible instructs us."

Emma looked up at the lovely man before her. She reached out her hand and touched his cheek.

"I'm so glad God has chosen you to be the head of our home."

"Shall we pray together, now?"

Emma nodded.

Roger reached out for her hands, prayed for their friends and committed their own future to the care and guidance of the Lord they loved.

Their conversation back to Green Pastures was animated and obviously centred around their forthcoming marriage.

"Would October be too soon to be married?"

"No, but I'd prefer just a simple wedding."

Amongst other things, Roger explained that as his year as a House Surgeon was almost complete his father had spoken about the possibility of coming into General Practice with him. Emma was delighted to learn that Roger had already accepted the offer. As his speciality was paediatrics Roger would concentrate mainly on the younger patients whilst Doctor John would continue to attend the older clientele.

"I think I would also like to look into the possibility of theatre work at the City hospital, one day a week. Just to keep my hand in!"

As they approached the Durrant's lovely home there was a lull in their conversation as they each thought of the oasis of peace this place had become. In a year that had commenced in so bleak and turbulent a manner it had witnessed many changing emotions, not least the work of grace in Emma and Roger's lives. The two hearts that were just setting out on a life's journey together acknowledged with wonder the instigator of this miracle, "It's all because of You, Lord."

Lightning Source UK Ltd.
Milton Keynes UK
UKOW03f1147111014

239938UK00002B/25/P